WHAT SKY WOMAN KNEW

WHAT
SKY WOMAN
KNEW

A NOVEL BY

DAVID FUSELIER

WHAT SKY WOMAN KNEW

BY DAVID FUSELIER

Editing by JoAnn Jolley
Cover Art: © Joe Therasakdhi

Read other books in the Sam Grant series:

A Fog on Spirit Island (2014)

Stars Like Diamonds (2015)

The Standing Bear (2016)

Feast of the Dead (2017)

Dancing Geese (2020)

Books are available from Amazon. Electronic versions are available for Kindle and compatible devices.

ISBN: 9798755110075

Printed in the USA

To Marian,
who fills all the holes in my life

PROLOGUE

NOT IN ALL his years had Charlie Weegwasi ever seen a spirit, but he had always known they were out there, all around, every day.

Most were probably those little forest spirits, what his Ojibwe called *bagwajiwinii*. He could hear them sometimes on windy nights, banging around on things. Sometimes they just tapped, like tap, tap, tap, tap. They probably learned that from the woodpecker, but Charlie wasn't fooled.

Damned little wild things is what they were, some of them no bigger than fleas that get up your nose and make you sick. But some the size of a gorilla, or even bigger. They'd steal things in the night, and the next day a bucket might be missing, or an axe. Then later it would turn up somewhere else.

Some people said they were the spirits of dead people who got lost after they died. Maybe the person wasn't buried right, under a spirit house, with his feet pointing west. If he had been buried right, all his spirit had to do was go the direction it was pointing for four days, down the path of souls to the Land of Peace. But if it got lost, it might just wander around the forest and get into mischief.

Sometimes when Weegwasi walked in the woods, he would catch movement from the side of his eye. But when he turned, there would be nothing there.

He had a theory about that, and he had told it to that big social worker when she came around from the Red Cliff tribal office. He told her that spirits could be quite big, but they had a way of making themselves thin as a sheet of paper. When you tried to look at them, they just turned sideways so you couldn't see them.

Tricky things they were, and it was unlikely you would ever see one until it came to get you. "They'll chase you if you run," he told her. "Best to just stand still and look dem right in da eye. Don't let dem get behind you."

She had nodded and smiled, but Weegwasi didn't think she cared much about spirits.

And now here was one right outside his window, looking in. Big yellow eyes and a nose like a bird. From the size of the head, he figured it was ten feet tall and had to stoop to see in the window.

Charlie moved around behind his old table that was painted buttermilk white maybe thirty years ago. It was a sturdy table, and it was the only thing he had to get behind. He crouched on his haunches so just his eyes were above the surface.

It was dark in his cabin, lit only by a kerosene lantern. Still, he could see those eyes plainly, see them through the dirt on the glass, through the falling snow, and through all that smoke outside that had blown in from those big forest fires out west. The eyes were big as donuts and evil-looking. They stared at him and never blinked.

"Go away!" he shouted. "Why are you here?"

When the big eyes never moved, he figured the spirit couldn't speak the white man's tongue, so he switched to the old language. *"Aaniin ezhinikaazoyan?"* he yelled out. *"Aandi wenjibaayan?* Who are you? Where did you come from?"

The monster struck the side of his cabin so hard the glass rattled. Then the eyes disappeared.

Charlie stayed right where he was and tried to remember all the spirits who had come to torment the people since Sky Woman fell. There were *Nibiinnaabe,* the water spirits, and *Memegwesi,* the spirit who destroys canoes. But they live in lakes and rivers.

Mishibizhiw, the giant panther, would have eyes like that. But he lives underwater, which is frozen in the Wisconsin winter.

Misigenebig, the horned serpent, might have eyes like that, too. Charlie shivered. The serpent eats people.

But it could be *Animikii,* the giant thunderbird. That wouldn't be so bad. But *Animikii* was rarely seen.

Biboon was the spirit of the north wind, and he was in a fury outside. But he was probably invisible.

It could be a rolling head monster. The heads emerge from the graves of men who have been hideously murdered, and they roll around seeking revenge.

Worst of all, it could be a *wiindigoog,* a vile creature created when an evil spirit possessed a corrupt man, someone who had sinned beyond redemption, who had committed incest or fed on human flesh, who had cheated or betrayed his family or his clan.

A person so possessed might, for a short time, just have a little fever or a chill. But every day the evil in him would grow. Eventually his body would start to change. He might double his size, but he would become so emaciated his spine would protrude from his back. He would run in a stoop. His long, spindly arms and legs would grow claws and his head antlers. His hunger could not be satisfied, and he would hunt anything human or animal.

The wind rattled the cabin and made the roof creak. He could hear things flapping outside. For a long time Charlie stayed behind the table, his teeth chattering. "I don't like dat dang," he whispered. Urine soaked his pants. He was an old man, and he couldn't help it.

He would not leave the spot behind the table even to feed wood into the stove, so the cabin was getting cold. About an hour before sunrise, he took the lantern to the door and opened it about an inch, trying not to make a sound. What if it was still there, whatever it was? He had a shotgun on the wall, but you cannot shoot a spirit.

He looked out with one eye. He didn't see anything, so he opened the door a little wider for his two eyes. Finally, he stuck his whole head out. The snow had stopped and the moon had emerged from the overcast, bright enough to throw shadows across the white winter blanket.

Charlie could see a line of huge tracks in the fresh white powder, coming out of the forest, coming down to the cabin, walking right across his porch, and then disappearing around the side. He looked down and studied the tracks. The hair on his neck bristled. Bumps crawled across his skin. The terror stopped his heart and made it hard to breathe.

The tracks were the size of watermelons, half human and half bird. Or maybe half bear. At any rate, they had claws, attached to a huge bare foot, a human foot, but twice the size. There was no doubt now. It was a *wiindigoog*, and it had come for Charlie Weegwasi.

ONE

THE RIVER had been friendly back then, a remote and lazy ribbon of tea, coiling through the lowland and marshes of the reservation. In the spring the steelhead had come up from the great lake to spawn, and in the fall the salmon and mackinaw. The bears and the eagles had come to meet them, and it had all seemed so friendly. But now it was frozen and buried in snow and surrounded by a new evil.

Sam Grant leaned against the open door of Harold Brebeuf's old cabin and wondered if the world would ever seem friendly again, wondered if he could ever get back the feeling. The love. The trust.

He was five when his grandmother had first brought him to the river, but he could remember the day with perfect clarity. Grandma had a trailer near the lakeshore at Red Cliff, where she was enrolled. But she had many relatives here at Bad River and she would bring him here, down to the river, to pull the trout from her fish traps.

Scattered stands of hemlock garnished the river bottom, and their tannin stained the water brown, but it was clear and the boy could see the big trout hovering above the multi-colored rocks, darting away when he threw a rock, then returning to precisely the same place.

The old memories glistened in his mind, bright and clear and perfect. He could not remember what he had done last week, yet he could remember every moment of his childhood.

The trailer had sat on tires and for many years looked ready to move on. But it never moved at all, and finally the tires had rotted and cracked and gone flat. The wheels had rusted, and the axles, and everything that was steel. But the aluminum had held up until his grandmother's death. Then the tribe had come in with a crane and hauled it off.

Grant staggered briefly against a sudden gust of wind, his bad leg still unsteady. Flakes of snow big as leaves floated by on the west wind. A foot had fallen overnight, on top of the foot from last week and another foot the week before.

Above the river bottom and the hemlock, on higher ground, a thick forest of big pine and hardwood was crowded by stands of young aspen, thin as broom handles, and scrub oak and raspberry.

Fifty years ago, Brebeuf had built his cabin here, on the high ground, clearing the trees out to fifty yards in every direction. He had left only the sugar maple and the biggest white pine and spruce. And now they were old too.

Standing off, halfway across the clearing, was the woodshed, buried in snow so it looked three feet tall, like an abode for dwarfs. Hoarfrost coated the roof and sides and all the trees and limbs around. Between the cabin and the shed, diamond dust rolled along the surface, frozen humidity, tiny crystals suspended in air too cold to tolerate liquid. When the sun peeked out, the diamonds threw a ring around it. Some turned to tiny prisms glinting yellow and blue and red.

Out beyond the diamonds and the shed and the rim of trees and the river was the disease, and the desolation of people who lived with masked faces that hid every smile, if there was one to hide. Out there were the closed schools, the shuttered businesses, unemployment, poverty, riots.

Grant had always carelessly loved the Earth, the way some men can love a woman who is fresh and bright and joyful, and in her heart a killer.

She was easy to love on sweet autumn days when the maples glow red in the sun. Or on the great lake when the wind fills the sail and lifts the boat and sends it gliding toward the low island penciled in the mist. Or near the fire at night, above the lake, when the banjo frogs and cicada sing and the sparks dance into the dark sky, and the smell of burning larch carries you back to your youth and family. You love her then too, and easily, and you don't think about the rest.

But she will kill you, like the others. That's what she does to her lovers, to 99.9 percent of all the species who have clung to her bosom. She wipes them clean, so you wouldn't know they were here, except for the fossils in the rocks and in the seabed, and the footprints stamped into a beach that turned to stone.

Massive storms, floods, eruptions, fires, droughts, acid oceans, poison air, molten lava. She has a hundred weapons in her arsenal, and already five mass extinctions on her record. Glaciations, asteroid impacts, wandering continents, colliding sheets of crust, unstable ocean levels.

And she has the microbes: the bacteria, fungi, prions, parasites, viruses. Her new disease was killing more Americans that winter than World War II, Korea and Vietnam combined, and effortlessly, without making a sound, like it was nothing.

It had only been 70,000 years since the last time she nearly killed us all. A mere beat of her heart. A few of us survived then, but she will finish the job someday. Maybe someday soon.

How can I love her now? Grant wondered. How can I ever love her again? Yet to live without that love seemed unthinkable. She nourishes. She gives meaning. A spirit un-nourished by nature is a spirit maimed. It is a cripple. An empty shell. It is the rind without the fruit inside, without the sweetness.

It is the senseless irony of things that you must love your killer.

When the Ojibwe hero Aayaash had found such a world, he had burned it down with a magic arrow, burned it down so it could begin again, so it could grow back better.

Grant sucked in the icy air and listened to the faint wet sound of snow falling lightly in perfect wilderness. There was nothing else but the low growl of wind. A soft world insulated in snow murmurs a kind of muted stillness.

Maybe we are all near the end of our time here, Grant thought. Or maybe it is just me who is near, and so I am too gloomy. I am just one old Indian in all this crushing white, and I am tired, and my body is all broken up.

Sky Woman must have seen the world coming to this, from the moment she fell through the hole in the sky. Why, then, did she leave her children here? Why did she abandon us in such a beautiful and deadly place? What did Sky Woman know?

"How are you today, Crow Eyes?" asked Brebeuf, who was bent over his old wood stove, poking into it with a stick. Smoke was rolling out into the room, causing him to wrinkle his deeply-lined old face. "You seem to be lost somewhere inside your head."

Grant took in one more good breath and plotted a route to the shed. He would have to step up from the porch onto the latest layer of snow, then cover the twenty yards between without falling through. He might be able to do that on snowshoes. The trouble was, the added weight of any wood he carried back would take him down.

"I should try to make it to the woodshed," Grant said without enthusiasm.

"We have enough for today."

"It may be more difficult tomorrow."

"The snow will stop now. The black-hat birds have moved away. The *mukadayostegwan banayshee*, I think. I have forgotten the word for them in the old language."

"The white people call them chickadees."

"They come when the snow is flying this way. They leave when the snow flies on. How is your head? Have you remembered that time you were hanged?"

"It is the same today as yesterday," Grant responded. "And the day before."

"I think a man who was hanged would remember. Maybe you had a stroke."

"My brain was without oxygen, Uncle. I guess it doesn't matter why."

"You are walking better, but your left leg still drags."

"I can live with it. The bad leg. The bad arm. And this damned, useless hand. I wish I could comb my hair."

"You look like a shipwreck survivor." The old man cackled and nodded. "Maybe not quite a survivor."

"I never realized how many things take two hands. Putting on pants and socks. Buttering bread. Pulling up a zipper."

"I think you will get better."

"I will get what I get. I think it would be good to go to the woodshed."

"Can you look down, or does it still make you dizzy?"

"Dizzy and sick. And now I have one eyelid that doesn't want to open. It is something new every day."

"Then you should not go," Brebeuf warned.

"I went Monday and I was fine."

"Monday there was half the snow. What if you fall? Who could help? I am older than you and so is Mrs. Brebeuf. And that is pretty old."

"You are a great shaman, my uncle. A fourth degree Midew. I am sure you would think of something."

"I am tired of thinking. Sleeping is better."

"Maybe you could find me a helping spirit. Wenebojo, maybe. Or Aayaash."

"You have your grandmother's spirit."

"We are not on speaking terms."

"Do you blame her for your troubles?"

"What she wanted for me was *Ninoododadiwin*."

"Yes. Harmony."

"Humility, also. She thought I was arrogant."

"Yes."

"Well, one cannot be arrogant who cannot tie his shoe," Grant observed.

"Does she not come to you anymore?"

"No."

"Not even in dreams?"

"Not since Paraguay."

"How do you feel about that?"

Grant closed the door and looked at the old man. "I am content."

"Do you want a lesson today?"

"I want to know about Muskrat."

"Tell me what you are thinking."

"The whole world was water when Sky Woman fell through the hole in the sky and landed on the back of the great turtle."

"Yes," Brebeuf confirmed as he was drawn into the conversation. "It was the second world after the first had been destroyed by the rising seas. Or maybe it was the third. Or the fourth. I cannot remember. One was destroyed by fire. Then there was the ice."

Grant picked up the story. "She asked each of the animals to dive to the bottom of the water and bring up a bit of dirt, so she could plant the turtle's back with the seeds she had brought down from the sky. But they all failed, every one of them, until Muskrat went down. He grabbed a handful of soil and came up with it, but he had gone so deep he died. With that little bit of dirt, clenched in his fist, she planted our world."

Brebeuf nodded. "Yes."

"But why Muskrat? He is not a diving animal, or important in any other way. He is rarely in other stories."

"Because even muskrats can be heroes."

"That's the easy thing to think. But what if the meaning of the story is different? Muskrat was not qualified to make that dive, and neither were the other animals. What if the story is telling us that the world is made, sometimes through great acts of heroism, by those who have absolutely no idea what they are doing?"

Brebeuf smiled. "Yes. Probably. But you must go deeper into each story we discuss."

"That's what I try to do."

"Deeper. Like Muskrat, until you reach the bottom. It is where the truth lives."

"Sky Woman was testing the animals to see if they and man could live together and help each other. She must have thought they could. Now I wonder."

"She gave birth on the turtle's back. On Turtle Island. Her children were the first Ojibwe. What does it mean to you that she chose to give birth, to bring her children into this new world?"

Just then Mrs. Brebeuf called from the kitchen, where she was working on the loom next to the wall behind a table with buckets and spiles for collecting maple sap. She sat with her back to Grant as he limped toward her. With her right hand and arm she was holding apart the beater bars. With her left she was holding up two broken pieces of carved aspen.

"Mr. Grant, I have broken my shuttle. Can you get me another? I can't let go of this. I think you will find one in the bottom drawer in the bedroom."

Grant shuffled back through the little living room and into the only bedroom. He kept a smile on his face so Brebeuf would not see the pain.

In the bedroom, he tried to look down at the drawer. Quickly, just a glance. But that was all it took to send him reeling. He stumbled forward against the dresser, but managed to hold himself up and choke back the nausea.

He stepped to the closet and pulled out an old wire hanger, which he reshaped into a long shaft with a hook on the end. Without looking down, he fumbled around until he got the hook into the handle of the bottom drawer. Then he leaned back against the rod and pulled the drawer open, pulled it too far actually, until the whole thing came out and dropped nosily to the wood plank floor.

He dropped the hanger and did a deep knee bend, keeping his head rigidly up, not daring even a peek downward. With his one good hand he felt around inside the drawer, trying to discover something that felt like a shuttle. But the drawer was full of things that didn't feel like that at all. He lifted some to his good eye so he could see. One was a round can of stove polish. Another was a leather bag full of beads.

"Uncle, could you come help, please?"

Brebeuf had plenty of infirmities of his own, but they were different than Grant's, and complementary. Grant could not look down, but Brebeuf's skinny little body was bent over into a permanent stoop. His head looked straight down all the time, which made him perfect for the task at hand. Brebeuf tottered over and looked down into the drawer while Grant touched and moved various things for his old uncle to see.

For a long time, Brebeuf grunted and groaned and strained his eyes. His long gray hair tumbled down around his face and he tried to push it away. "I cannot see without my glasses."

"Where are they?"

"The missus is using them to weave."

"You have only one set of glasses for the two of you?"

"They do not grow on trees."

"Wait here."

Grant got himself up with difficulty and went back to the kitchen to borrow the glasses right off Mrs. Brebeuf's head. Back in the bedroom, Mr. Brebeuf had reached down as far as he could and just snagged the top of the leather bag. It fell onto the floor and a thousand little beads scattered in every direction just as Grant walked in. His feet flew from under him and he landed hard on his butt, holding on to the only pair of glasses like they were a nuclear trigger.

"Are you okay?" Brebeuf asked. Grant took a couple of deep breaths and said yes, he thought so. "You should be more careful," the old man said.

"What was that?" Mrs. Brebeuf hollered out, sounding alarmed.

"Nothing, dear," her husband said. "We are getting you a shuttle."

"I could have made one by now," she huffed.

Grant turned onto his knees and, keeping his head up, crawled back to the drawer and handed Brebeuf the glasses. Together they found the shuttle and Grant pulled himself back to his feet by grasping the bedspread and blankets and sheets. In the process, all the freshly-made bed linen ended up in a heap on the floor.

Taking Brebeuf by the arm, he guided the old man into the living room and sat him down, exhausted, in the recliner. Grant took the shuttle into Mrs. Brebeuf, who did not say thank you, and turned to go out the kitchen door where there were snowshoes on the porch. He was thinking it was a good time to get out of there, but Mrs. Brebeuf called him back.

"Mr. Grant, I cannot work without the glasses." Grant spun on his one good leg and limped back into the living room.

"The mailman is here," she shouted.

Mr. Brebeuf was asleep in the recliner, so Grant just removed the glasses and shambled to the window. Outside, up to its fenders in snow, was a new pickup truck with chains on the tires. It had a big plow blade in front and had pushed out a path all the way down the long lane and across the clearing to the cabin. Getting out was Bayfield County Sheriff Lewis Radisson, way out of his county and his jurisdiction. He had removed his big black gun belt, and without it he was just a regular man in a freshly-pressed uniform.

"It's a friend of mine," Grant said, taking the glasses into Mrs. Brebeuf.

"Well, tell him to come in and have a cookie. He can leave the mail on the flour bin. Tell him not to track snow."

"I'm going outside to talk with him." Grant took his coat down from the hook and was half out when he turned to the woman and asked softly, "Mrs. Brebeuf, are you feeling okay?"

"Yes," she said. "I'm sorry. I'm kind of snarly this morning."

"Well, it's up to you, of course. But I think it would be best if you didn't go into the bedroom until you are in a better frame of mind."

TWO

"YOU ARE one hard man to find," Radisson said. "I thought you had bought a house in Ashland. Then someone said you were living out here on the Bad River Reservation."

The men did not shake hands because it was no longer acceptable. Radisson wore a mask to keep his *bagwajiwinii*, if he had any, from jumping out of his nose and onto other people. Grant did not have a mask, so he kept his distance. He did not know how far a *bagwajiwinii* could jump, but supposed a particularly athletic one might be good for several feet.

"Man, this is the middle of nowhere," Radisson said, looking around. "At least the snow has stopped."

"No," Grant said. "She is just reloading."

"It must be a mile off the road. I used my GPS but even so I couldn't find the lane in here. Nothing has been plowed and there are no tire tracks. Where's your truck?"

"I don't know. I left it somewhere."

"You left it somewhere?"

"Maybe in my garage. Maybe at Walmart. Maybe somewhere else. I don't remember."

"Sam, are you okay?"

"I have a sore back. I'm sleeping every night in Mr. Brebeuf's recliner."

"Why don't you go home?"

"I lost my truck."

Radisson narrowed his eyes and scanned Grant from top to bottom.

"You look like crap. Worse even than when you got back from Paraguay. I thought you'd be better by now."

"Maybe a little."

"Can't you comb your hair?"

"Lewis, I'm going to braid it. Just as soon as I grow another hand."

"How is your brain?"

"Half of it is amazing."

"You can't drive?"

"Sure. But I can't look down. I get dizzy."

"We should find your truck. Let's go see if it's in your garage."

"Let's not."

"Why, Sam?"

"It's a long story."

"I drove all the way here from Washburn, in the snow."

"Well, I can't look down, so when I was making toast, I held the toaster up to my eyes so I could look in. The popper-upper doesn't always work and you have to watch the toast or it will burn." Radisson waited as Grant gathered more thoughts. "Well, the popper worked and the toast flew out and hit me in the eyes."

"Is that why your one eye is closed?"

"No, that's something else. What happed was the toast fell onto the floor in the pantry where I keep the toaster. There is a shelf and a plug in there so the toaster doesn't clutter the counter."

"I see."

"Well, I got down on my knees and started feeling around on the floor for the toast, and I hit the button that turns on the vacuum cleaner."

Radisson chuckled.

"So, there I was with toast crumbs in my eyes. I am trying to find my toast and turn off the vacuum cleaner, and somehow I get my arm through the cord and I pull the toaster down on my head."

"Good Lord."

"It hurt, so I got mad and grabbed the thing and kind of threw it down. The old cord snapped just an inch or two away from the plug. It started shooting sparks. And smoking too. A lot.

"But I keep a fire extinguisher right there in the kitchen, so I got it and pulled the lever, and this foam stuff started shooting all over the place. I couldn't get it to shut off with my one good hand. The foam just kept coming until the thing was empty. It filled up the whole pantry and half the kitchen. It was up to my knees. It was a terrible mess."

Grant nodded and seemed to think he was finished, seemed to think it was now clear what had happened to his truck.

"We'll clean it up when we get there," Radisson said comfortingly. "What does that have to do with your truck?"

"I cleaned it up the next day," Grant said. "Got the plug out, too. But it had blown a fuse and the fridge wasn't working. I have forty pounds of venison in there."

"What about your truck?"

"It's an old house and has one of those old fuse boxes that use round fuses, the kind you screw in."

"My house does too."

"I didn't have any of those fuses, so I put a penny in the hole and screwed in the old fuse and that worked fine. Fridge came right on."

"That's dangerous, my friend."

"Well, it was fine that night and all the next day. About six o'clock I decided to go to Walmart and get a fuse and a new fire extinguisher. I walked out the front door and my truck wasn't there. Then I thought, hey, maybe I put it in the garage. So I came back in and opened the door to the garage."

"And your truck wasn't there?"

"I don't know, because when I looked over at the kitchen, the whole wall behind the fridge and the stove was kind of melting. The paint was blistering and falling right off. Then the wall started swelling, and pretty soon flames started coming out all over the place."

"On no. Sam…"

"And my fire extinguisher was empty."

"Did you call 911?"

"I thought of that as soon as I got outside. But I had left my phone inside, I guess. I didn't know where it was. But my neighbor called for me."

"Were you able to save much? How long did it take for the trucks to get there?"

"I'm not sure. Maybe an hour."

"Sam! They're just a few blocks away."

"I know. But my neighbor wasn't home. He was over at Ed's Place. The bar. So I had to walk over there."

"Oh Sam…"

"But when I got there, he was putting the moves on some woman, so I thought I'd better wait a bit. Maybe have a Leinie."

"You paused for a beer?"

"It was a long walk."

"Oh, dear God."

"By the time my neighbor and I got back close to my home, it was getting dark and the whole sky was glowing yellow and red. It was real pretty."

"Oh Sam. I'm so sorry. You burned your house down."

"Oh no," Sam said. "It burned itself down, and, may I say, with wonderful enthusiasm."

"Wonderful?"

"Lewis, I don't know a lot about house fires, but it seems to me that was a very happy fire. It was an old house and I think that fire had been waiting a long time to burn it down. It danced around the roof like a young puppy. You should have seen it."

Radisson sighed deeply. "And your truck was in the garage?"

"Maybe. Or maybe it was at Walmart. I've been trying to walk more, to get back in shape, and sometimes I walk to Walmart and back."

"So… you think you may have driven over there and forgot you drove and walked home?"

"Yes," Grant nodded confidently. "Or maybe at the Goodwill."

"What are you going to do about your house?"

"Oh, it's all taken care of. The insurance company is going to give me a bunch of money."

"Will you rebuild?"

"No. The policeman who came said I was a danger to myself. A social worker came and brought me out here to Brebeuf's. The insurers are keeping the lot and cleaning it up and putting it up for sale. I got the idea the neighbors don't really want me back."

"I suppose."

"And the company didn't want to insure another house."

"Did you lose everything? All your clothes and stuff? Did you have lots of old pictures of you and your family?"

"I don't remember."

"Really?"

"Why did you come, Lewis?"

"I wanted to ask for your help, but ... well, never mind."

"No. I can help. What? I would like to help."

"I'm sorry, Sam. I don't think you're able. I wanted to ask you about Charlie Weegwasi, over on the Red Cliff Reservation."

"Yes. What about him?"

"He is missing."

"Maybe he is with my truck."

Radisson looked down and kind of coughed. "It's okay, Sam. I'll figure it out." He turned and walked toward his pickup. "Goodbye, Sam. Take care of yourself. I'm sorry about your house. I hope you get better."

"Thanks for coming, Sheriff."

Radisson got in and was just about to close the truck door when Grant hollered, "You don't have jurisdiction in Red Cliff." Radisson looked at him and waited. "But Weegwasi doesn't live on the reservation. He is enrolled, but he lives on his own land. One hundred and sixty acres right adjacent. If he's missing, I guess it's your case."

Radisson climbed out. "Sam, are you putting me on? Is this some kind of act? It's just the sort of crazy stunt you would pull."

"What act?"

"Did you really burn your house down?"

"Why do you think I am sleeping on a recliner?"

"I am going to ask you again, Sam. Where is your truck?"

Grant looked down, then up, then side to side. He squinted and thought for a long time. "I think someone stole it," he said.

Radisson leaned back against his hood and sighed again. "Why did you stop for a beer at that bar? Tell me the truth."

Grant cleared his throat and looked away. "I guess, for a little while, I forgot why I had gone there."

"Uh-huh. That's what I thought."

Grant gathered himself up and looked straight into his old friend's eyes. "Lewis," he said, "I think I am a little better. But I am a little older. They kind of cancel each other out."

"I can see that."

"I want to help. It's been so long. So long since that time in Paraguay. And Jeannie ... well, I would like to feel useful again."

Radisson seemed unconvinced.

"Help me be useful again, Lewis. Please."

THREE

GRANT WATCHED the white world roll by outside and he was happy to be in Radisson's new truck, even if he had to wear the mask. He was happy to be away from the tiny house in the woods and happy to be doing something. "The last time I saw Charlie Weegwasi, you had him in jail for murder."

"That wasn't me, Sam. That was the FBI wanted him there. I'm the one who let him out. Against their advice. At great risk to my career and reputation, such as they are."

Grant cleared his throat.

"Anybody could see that old man was harmless. But he had kind of confessed."

Grant and Radisson were on their way to Ashland to look for Grant's truck and then decide what to do. Grant used his good right arm to grasp the handle above the passenger door. Using it for leverage, he readjusted his position on the seat because his back hurt. The handle snapped off in his hand.

"Huh," he said, looking at the handle. "That's kind of funny."

"Sam Grant, you are a walking disaster," Radisson growled.

"Limping. I am a limping disaster. To be a walking disaster is my goal in life."

"Well, you've got the disaster part mastered. This is a brand-new truck."

"It is not a good omen."

After a very long silence, as Grant looked at the broken handle in his hand and wondered what to do with it, he said softly, "I think later you will see it was funny."

"Can we get back to Weegwasi? I'd like to accomplish something as a result of this crazy trip that burned a tank of gas and muddied my truck and broke it to boot."

"Weegwasi did not confess. You are too *Wabiska*. Too white. Charlie is very traditional."

"Well, right now, he is very missing."

"You asked him if he had killed that man and he told you that it was possible. He had heard that there was Lyme disease in deer, which he figured was little *bagwajiwinii,* little evil spirits, that moved from the deer's blood to your blood. Since he had just butchered a deer, he thought it was possible he had gotten some *bagwajiwinii* into him and they had made him murder that man."

"My God…"

"But he was just admitting to the possibility, that's all. He didn't remember doing it. But he believed in spirits and didn't want to rule it out."

"You mean he actually thought a spirit might have made him kill someone and then not remember it?"

"Well, yes."

"Sweet Jesus."

"Do you believe in miracles, Lewis?"

"No, I don't. Well, some maybe. I don't know."

"Miracles exist all around us. Children emerge from one tiny, fertilized cell. Electrons pop in and out of existence. Salamanders come back to the place they were born from many miles away. A traditional Ojibwe is sensitive to the mysteries of nature."

"The mystery I'm interested in is what happened to Charlie Weegwasi. I'll tell you the truth, Sam. I don't know where to begin."

"I can help."

"Can you? It would be wonderful if you could. I have that plane crash to deal with and a dozen other things. I mean, if you think your mind is up to … you know."

"Yarrow, what we call Squirrel Tail, can be thrown into a fire, and the smoke will cure a headache."

"What?"

"Cat's Foot tea will help a new mother expel the afterbirth and heal inside. Thistle helps stomach cramps. Goldenrod will cure spasms. Dandelion tea for heartburn. Dogwood bark to cause vomiting. Bunchberry for colic. Horsetail for dropsy."

"You're scaring me, Sam."

"Wintergreen tea for pain. Do you know it contains the same chemicals as aspirin?"

"Really?"

"Lewis, I can remember every single thing my grandmother told me when I was a child. I suddenly know the names and uses of probably two hundred plants and roots and barks. I can tell you where to find them and how to prepare them. Isn't that amazing? I didn't even know I knew them."

"You are remembering things you had forgotten?"

"Songs. Stories. Dances. It's all coming back. I can tell you how to make a drum or find the roots used to sew up birch bark canoes. I can clearly remember things that happened when I was barely old enough to walk."

"But you don't know where you left your truck?"

"Not a clue."

"What else don't you remember?"

Grant sighed. "Let's see. Hardly anything in Paraguay. Not much since. I remember the house fire."

"Do you remember what you ate yesterday?"

Grant laughed. "Lewis, I don't remember IF I ate yesterday."

"I think that happens when you have Alzheimer's. You can't remember new things, but old things become more vivid. Your problem may not be just the hanging. We need to get you to a doctor. A neurologist."

"I have already called. It is a four-month wait."

"You're kidding."

"Apparently there is a thriving market in lame brains."

"I'm sorry, Sam."

"No. It's all right. If I had to choose between remembering the new stuff or remembering the old stuff, I would take the old stuff. There's not much new in my life that's worth remembering."

"I understand. You weren't able to get Jeannie to come home. And then you burned down your house."

"No, I chose to have toast. Everything after that was inevitable. It's wonderful, Lewis, really. I don't just remember my lessons as a child; I can suddenly see the connective tissue of life, how things interrelate. It's like autism. I can't remember details, but I can see patterns I have never seen before."

"Huh."

"I bought the house hoping Jeannie would come back. If I hadn't bought it, I wouldn't have burned it down. But that's not the beginning either. When I decided a year ago to return to Paraguay, I sealed the fate of that old house. I can see it all so clearly."

"Can you see what happened to Charlie Weegwasi?"

"Who?" Grant asked blankly. Radisson rolled his eyes and sighed. "I'm just kidding, Lewis. Tell me what you know."

FOUR

IT WAS Weegwasi's grandson who called the tribal police. They referred the case to Bayfield County. The grandson said he went for a visit and Charlie wasn't home. There was no fire in the stove and the cabin was ice cold. There were no tracks because of all the new snow. The grandson visits about every two weeks, and two weeks ago everything seemed fine. Charlie had no phone or electricity and did not drive anymore. Neighbors would drive in and take him to the store when he hung a plastic bag on his mailbox.

Radisson had talked to those helpful neighbors, but nobody had seen Weegwasi in weeks. "They weren't worried because he typically stores a lot of food and has dried venison and such," Radisson said. "They say he hunts, too. Mostly rabbits in the winter, but also deer. I went to the house and there were no signs of a struggle."

"Was his rifle still in the cabin?"

"First thing I checked. There was a double-barrel shotgun and a .44 Ruger carbine with a scope. Doesn't mean he didn't go off hunting with another gun. But it means he wasn't robbed. There wasn't much of value in the house, but any thief would have taken the firearms."

"I can't believe he would have gone hunting in this weather. How about snowshoes?"

Radisson shrugged. "Didn't see any. Can't say I looked everywhere. They could be outside buried in the snow."

"Was there food left out? Did it look like he had planned to come right back?"

"Everything was fine. It looked like an old cabin that belonged to an old man. It was neat, but pretty empty. There were lots of scraps of wood and fur and things like porcupine quills. Nothing else stood out. There was no note."

"He can't read or write."

Radisson nodded. "See, those are the kinds of things that I need to know. I need to know who he is and what he does. How he makes a living. Whether he has a mattress full of cash. A life insurance policy. I need to know who inherits his property. Who stands to gain by his death … or his disappearance."

"You're looking for a motive."

"Of course. It's probably a simple case: an old guy wandered off into the winter and died of exposure. We'll find him next spring when the snow melts. But I have to rule out foul play. Until I can do that, it's an open case. How did he manage to buy all that land? That's unusual, isn't it?"

"Red Cliff is a pretty small reservation," Grant explained. "Tribal members who do well will sometimes buy land nearby, where they can stay in touch. They often leave that land to the tribe when they die."

"You think he did that?"

"I will find out."

"Thank you. You know I have no legal authority to ask for anything from the tribal government. The FBI can do that, but they won't step in unless it's clear there was a federal crime. And anyway, they're busy with that plane crash."

"I understand. Were there any baskets in the house?"

"Let's see. He had a big one with kindling in it. I think a little one with matches. Lots of matches. He had candles and kerosene lanterns everywhere."

"I mean new baskets. Just-made baskets. Ready to sell."

"Not that I noticed. Why?"

"It's what he did … or does. He is a basket maker. That's probably how he bought the land."

"By making baskets?"

"Charlie Weegwasi is the best Ojibwe basket maker in North America. His baskets are very unique."

"And you can buy 160 acres by making baskets?"

"I saw one of his for sale on eBay for $7,000.

"You're kidding."

"Of course he doesn't get that. That is the value on the secondary market, among collectors. I think he sells everything he makes at the Red Cliff summer powwow. But collectors come from all over the country. They'll pay $1,500 for a Weegwasi original. Maybe $2,500 for a really special one."

"My God, Sam. I never knew."

Grant nodded. "We'll add that to the list."

"That changes everything. It throws the case wide open. There's plenty of motive." Radisson let his mind turn for a bit. "Someone could have knocked him on the head and stolen the baskets. They might have done it outside or he might have crawled outside afterwards. If he's dead, I bet his body is right there near the cabin, under the snow. If I can find a body, I can determine a cause of death."

"I take it you weren't going to search?"

"His place is in the middle of nowhere, and there's like three feet of snow. You could be standing right on top of him and not know it. How many baskets are we talking about?"

"Making the baskets doesn't take long. But the traditional way of doing it is very difficult and labor intensive. You have to strip the wood from a Black Ash tree, which takes a lot of skill. There's a special way to do it by cutting and pounding the bark with a small club.

"You dye the wood using natural plants and minerals, like Bloodroot and iron. Then you dig up these thin little special roots from a White Spruce to tie it all together. That's really hard. You dig around near a tree until you find a proper little root, then you excavate it, following it through the soil. You don't want to break it.

"Maybe you decorate with quills and claws and antlers and fur, whatever you can find. The whole process takes time. And he is pretty old. I would be surprised if he is making more than thirty baskets a year. Maybe two or three a month."

"So, since the powwow, he could have made maybe twenty. That's like $30,000 worth of baskets. They should have been there at his place, and they weren't." Radisson was nodding and thinking. "If he's right there near the cabin, it's a lot easier. We'll start tomorrow. Bring in some dogs."

Radisson was happy to have a mission. He had been groomed for that by nearly twenty years in the Army Special Forces. He wasn't good at starting things, but he was a great finisher. "I'd say $30,000 is motive enough for murder."

"I think it's more like $60,000," Grant mused. "If Weegwasi is dead, or stays missing, and doesn't make any more baskets, the value of all his baskets goes way up. Collectors will double their money. Or triple it."

"My God. There's another motive. And a whole bunch of suspects. Are there big collectors?"

"Probably half a dozen rich people. That's the way it usually works. Most people own one or two. A lot of Ojibwe, for instance. But there are always a handful of those people who don't know what to do with all their money, and so they collect things. A savvy buyer who snatched up the best baskets when Charlie was in his prime could have a million-dollar collection. Some museums, too."

Radisson whistled. "Can we find out who they are?"

"I know an art dealer in Taos who handles a lot of Native American art. I'll give him a call."

But Grant was thinking that the kind of person who collects traditional Ojibwe baskets isn't exactly the type to bash an old man on the head. There was probably no foul play at all. But if there was a crime, it was terrible beyond measure. It was the kind of crime that could have only been done by a *wiindigoog*, a broken spirit who had become so corrupt he would attack the most helpless and innocent of men.

FIVE

THE BURNED remains of the Ashland house were hard to look at, and Grant turned away. Radisson was kind enough not to say anything.

"It wasn't exactly my dream house," Sam whispered. "But I bought it hoping Jeannie would come back. At least for visits. I knew she wouldn't come back as long as I was living in Bayfield. She's a big-city woman. She can't live in a town without a real grocery store."

"What do you hear from her?"

"Not much. She's still in Chicago. Still working. When I call, it's chitchat. Updates on old friends and her family. That's it."

"You've been separated for a long time, ever since your daughter was killed. It doesn't look very promising to me."

"No."

"Maybe you should close that door and move on."

"I can't do that until she does. And she never quite closes it."

"It's not healthy, Sam."

"Well, hell, Lewis. Look at me. Would you come back … to this?"

Radisson looked at him and started to say something, then he started to say something else. In the end, he said nothing at all.

Grant leaned back against the seat and sighed again. "It was a crazy idea. Ashland is not my home. I suppose I'll move back to Bayfield. When I can."

"Do you still have that place above the garage? I always liked it."

"I guess. I still pay the rent. But I can't get up and down those stairs."

Radisson got out of the truck and looked at the charred remains of Grant's house. About half of it had been cleared away by a large front-end loader that was still there, but nobody was in sight.

"You want to go dig around?" Radisson asked, leaning in the open window. "See if you can salvage anything?"

"Oh, God no. Thank you. I don't own enough stuff to worry about. The most valuable things in there were probably pictures. Of Jeannie and me and our girl. I'm sure they are all gone. And my computer. Nothing else matters."

"It doesn't look to me like there was a truck in that garage. Let's look around for it."

They started at Goodwill and went on to the dollar store and then Walmart. The truck was there, safe and sound. And Grant's phone was inside.

"Are you sure you can drive?" Radisson asked for the third time.

"I'll be fine. I just can't look down. I can get back to Brebeuf's, now that you've plowed it. It will be nice to have a vehicle and a phone. I feel better just thinking about it."

"I'll get some deputies out tomorrow to start searching for Weegwasi. I'll call if there is anything new."

"I'll check with the tribal office," Grant offered, and I'll keep my one good eye on the internet auction sites. If a bunch of Weegwasi baskets start showing up, we'll know what happened."

"I might need you to run interference for me on that plane crash, too. We're just getting no cooperation from the tribal people. Nobody will talk."

"What's the deal? I heard about it. I thought it was just one small plane that crashed on the ice, the pilot and the one passenger killed."

"That's how it started. I wasn't involved because the tribal police were on the scene first and they called the BIA and the FBI and then the FBI called the FAA, the DEA and the ATF. I'm telling you, it was alphabet soup around that plane."

"I don't get it."

"Well, it turned out the plane didn't exactly crash. It had skis and was landing on the snow, right in Raspberry Bay, up on the northern tip of the reservation."

"I grew up near there. Engine trouble?"

"Nope. The plane and pilot were from Canada, and illegally in the U.S."

"Drug runners?"

"No dope was found. The plane was taxiing in when it hit some bad snow or something and went nose-down. The prop broke off and the front of the plane, engine and everything, was pushed back into the cockpit. That killed the passenger, but it's not what killed the pilot."

"Really."

"The autopsy came back today. The pilot was killed after the crash by ..." Radisson scratched his head, squinted, and tried again to make sense of it. "He was hit on the head, possibly by something like a little axe or a hatchet or ... " Radisson cleared his throat. "Or maybe a tomahawk."

SIX

THE WATER that Jacob Dewberry wrung from his brand-new tactical pants was, as Mark Twain would have said, too thick to drink and too thin to plow. A full day on your knees in four feet of snow and slush and mud will do that. He wasn't the sort to care.

Dewberry was now, officially, a full-time patrol officer and evidence technician for the Red Cliff Band of the Chippewa Nation, or Ojibwe Nation, or the Anishinaabe Nation or First Nation or whatever it was today. What he cared about was that he had a job, and in the middle of a pandemic. It didn't pay much, and he was unsure whether it was the kind of job that might transform him into a chick magnet. But it was what he had always wanted to be: a person of some standing among his people.

He was born to the Loon Clan, in North America's largest native tribe. His father was from the Crane Clan, which meant he was supposed to be a leader. But at five foot eight, 165 pounds, Dewberry didn't leave much of a wake. He had the tightly-packed body of a runner, all-state in high school. And he was, as his mother had noted, Hollywood handsome. But he was one of those non-descript men who disappeared into crowded parties. He wasn't good at small talk. Didn't know a lot of people. Was quiet around women and slipped through life pretty much unnoticed. And then there was the name. How many great leaders do you know who were named Dewberry?

Maybe the uniform would help, if he could get it presentable again. It was a gift from Chief of Police Larry Lawrence, the only gift he was ever likely to get from a man who was stingy even with his words. "Here," the chief had said. "The next one's on you." That was the formal presentation. The other officers had applauded for at least four seconds.

And so Dewberry's career had begun, six months ago, as a probational part-timer. Last week he was bumped to full-time on the condition he quit his two-nights-a-week job as a blackjack dealer at the tribal casino. He had been hired there a year ago and had actually dealt blackjack for a total of twenty-one days, which he found ironic. Then the table games were all shut down for the duration of the pandemic, and Dewberry was without duties. But he had been kept on the payroll at a negligible level as the result of some government program.

Now he was in the position of having to resign from a job he had never really done, but for which he had been paid during the better part of a year.

He spent the day trying to figure out exactly how he was going to do that. He didn't even know his boss, or if he had one. It was all complicated, and it kept his mind busy while he rummaged around in the snow at the site of a small, single-engine plane crash on a frozen tribal bay in Lake Superior.

He was doing that as part of his responsibility as official Red Cliff evidence technician, a title he had won as the result of taking a 40-hour course in Basic Evidence

Technician School at the Milwaukee County Sheriff's office.

Thinking back on that course, it didn't seem to him that any of his instructors had anticipated his first assignment would be in fifty-one inches of snow, blown around like pellets in a forty-mile-an-hour gale. The only way to get around was on the department's snowmobile or on his knees, hunkered down as far has he could get into the snow, using it for shelter.

Farther out on the lake, the wind had scoured the ice and blown the snow toward shore, where it had piled up against the trees that lined the bay. The drifts were probably six feet deep against the first line of hemlock and larch, but tapered to a foot or two a quarter-mile out.

The plane was wrecked nose-down, its prop twisted, its windscreen shattered. The engine compartment and front cockpit were a mess. Both the pilot and passenger had been killed and their bodies removed.

The back two-thirds of the plane was in showroom condition. It had been a nice plane, a tail-dragger with skis on the front wheels.

Dewberry had flown such a plane and had landed it on the ice at Lac Court Oreilles, the 100-square-mile reservation on which he had grown up, ninety miles south of Red Cliff. He was sixteen at the time. His uncle was ten years older, a flyer, a drinker, a Romeo, and the principal reason Dewberry had never graduated from high school.

To escape the many bad influences of tribal life, his parents had hauled him to the Army recruiting office in Eau Claire and had hovered over him while he signed the papers. The Army was not accepting seventeen-year-old high school dropouts, but Dewberry was an Indian, an athlete and, according to all the tests, off-the-chart smart. He had wanted to join the Air Force, but his dad was pretty clear that the Ojibwe were warriors, not birds, and did not belong in the sky with *Migizi*, the eagle.

The army required Dewberry to attend school right after basic and get his GED, which he did, before two tours in Afghanistan as a fire support specialist.

Four years later he was in Red Cliff as a part-time cop and now, here he was, a full-time cop and evidence technician, wallowing around in the snow like a musk ox.

The plane was off-limits to anyone so humble as to be employed by Indians. It was there for the scholars from the FFA, and for the many degreed people who worked for a real government.

His instructions were clear: he was not to approach the plane, but he didn't think that barred him from tunneling into it under the snow. He wanted to get a look at the wheels, because ski planes have a pump mounted inside that forces the skis downward, below the level of the wheels. A pilot who forgets to pump could end up like that, nose-down. Maybe.

Burrowing down through the snow, Dewberry found one of the skis heavily damaged but apparently in the proper position for a snow landing. Why would the ski be damaged by a landing on four feet of snow? Maybe because it was wrecked when the plane turned nose-down and smashed up the front end. But the other ski was fine. Something didn't make sense.

Accompanying Dewberry on this frigid mission was Bearbait Bodette, another junior officer a year younger than Dewberry. When Jacob had asked Chief Lawrence why everyone called him Bearbait, he got a quick and gruff response. "Because he's not good for anything else."

It seemed cruel at the time, but Dewberry had come to understand. Bodette had a wonderful heart, something every police officer should have. But he was absolutely dumb as dirt. His two saving graces were kindness and unparalleled self-knowledge. Bearbait knew he was dumb, knew it wasn't his fault and knew there was not one thing he could do about it. So he flitted happily through life, finding ways to turn the most tedious assignments, like traffic diversion, into a romping good time.

He was wonderful company, and Dewberry loved their time together. Bodette would do anything you asked, and do it immediately. And when you weren't asking, he would be out of your way doing something totally frivolous and childish and fun. On this day he was building a snow ramp to see how far he could jump the department's snowcat.

Dewberry invested four or five more hours crawling through the snow, looking for anything that might have fallen off, any little part, anything. The blowing snow might have buried a key piece of evidence in a matter of minutes, and if he could find it, he might momentarily become a hero, and he might subsequently get a date with Janice Somebody who was interning in the health clinic. He didn't know her last name. Not yet. But she was cute and young and shorter than him, the three things he demanded. Of course he would have settled for two of them. Or even one.

Blowing and drifting snow had obscured any tracks of the landing and any sign of human involvement. Dewberry knew a dozen investigators and technicians had been here yesterday and tramped around for most of the day. Yet every trace of them was already gone.

But Jacob Dewberry knew snow, and he knew the big city agents did not. He had grown up in it, played in it, shoveled it on pretty much every day of every winter. While the surface could change in a few minutes, the lower layers preserved their history. Indeed, as more snow fell and added weight, the lower levels were compressed and hardened like layers of soft rock, locking in the stories they wanted to tell. The trick was to work snow like an archaeologist, going down layer by layer. That's why he had brought the trowel.

A cross section of months-old snow is laden with information. You could see when the temperature changed, how cold it got, and when it warmed up again. You could tell when it was windy and when it was still. You could even tell when the wind was from the south because it carried in a tint of fine soot from the coal and wood chips burned by the old power plant in Ashland.

Snow was a clock that recorded events in chronological order. Of course, reading that clock is a little harder in a northeast gale. But Dewberry persevered, his concentration occasionally interrupted by a revving engine and then squeals of delight.

Some people thought Jacob Dewberry was shy, but that was because he lacked any normal portion of self-promotion. He had no interest in rank or acclaim or even acceptance. He just wanted to learn stuff. He was perfectly comfortable with everything he was and was not. He was equipped with his own guidance system, his own goals, his own values and his own motives. He hadn't borrowed any of them from other people, and there was nobody whose approval he coveted.

Well, except maybe Janice Somebody. He was a man, after all, a young and healthy man, and had the usual set of needs. Several times in his life he had been smitten by such a woman. Maybe it was the way she had looked or walked. Or maybe her voice or the flash of her eyes. He was never quite sure. But he would be almost instantly enchanted and would spend long nights in lovely fantasy, constructing an imaginary life with a largely imaginary woman he had never actually met.

Back at his trailer, he was drying off and warming up and thinking what to do. He had forgotten all about his casino job and the need to resign. He had a much bigger issue now. He had found something that might indeed make him a hero. The problem was, he couldn't tell a soul. Not even the chief.

SEVEN

BREBEUF SCATTERED tobacco in the four directions, as he always did before what Sam Grant called a "lesson." Then he unrolled the long, soft cloth and took out the ceremonial pipe.

They sat on the porch that was covered by a roof made of just thin aspen poles laid side by side. It was good for shade from the sun, but snow filtered through and Grant had shoveled the porch the best he could.

Brebeuf took a puff on the pipe and blew the smoke upward, a tribute to the sun, the source of all life. Then he blew one down to Mother Earth, in whose womb we live. The last four puffs went to each of the four directions: to the east, the beginning place, where the sun rises and where life begins; to the west, the ending place, where the sun sets and where the deceased spirits go to the Land of Peace; to the north, the winter place, the source of hardship and struggle; and to the south, the summer place, where there is always joy and fun and plenty.

Brebeuf chanted as he smoked, and Grant listened for the meaning. Ojibwe songs and chants originally had lyrics in the old language, and many still do. But over the centuries, some songs had become just incoherent sounds. Brebeuf was always careful to use the original lyrics when they were known, or to use lyrics he created to fit the occasion, much as a Christian minister might do in a prayer.

This chant was about First Bear, who had come to First Woman and First Man, the children of Sky Woman. The mother had returned to her place in the sky and the children, alone now on Turtle Island, were starving. So the bear offered himself, his life, his sweet meat, so that they could live. It was the beginning of the first totem, *Doodem Makwa*, the Bear Clan, which would always be the healers and the defenders of the tribe. Six other clans would follow: The Crane and Loon clans, which supplied the orators and all the chieftains; the Martin Clan, the pipe bearers, the hunters and the food gatherers; the Fish Clan, the scholars and teachers; the Deer Clan, responsible for good housing and recreation; and the Bird Clan, the spiritual leaders.

When it was Grant's turn, he blew smoke in the same manner, but he did it absently. He didn't care about the Earth anymore and didn't want to honor it. He did a chant about Aayaash, the mythical hero, and how he had been saved by the Horned Serpent.

Then began the lesson, which always consisted of questions Grant could not usually answer, followed by an old story he had heard a hundred times. But Brebeuf was always keen to tell the stories.

"Let us begin today with the questions," Brebeuf said. "Are you going to help that sheriff know what happened to Weegwasi?"

"I think so. I need something to do."

"When you think such things, you get into trouble."

"I do," Grant laughed. "Look at me."

"I have known Charlie Weegwasi for many years. But I cannot afford his baskets. What do you think happened to him?"

"I don't know."

"You haven't seen? In your dreams?"

"No. I haven't really tried."

"Are you now afraid of the spirits? Do you hide from them?"

"I haven't thought about it."

"You might believe they have drawn away from you. But maybe you have drawn away from them."

"Maybe. Have YOU seen anything?"

"It is important that I ask the questions. Why are you here, Crow Eyes, here on my porch?"

"Because my house burned down and you were kind enough ... "

"Why are you here?" the old man interrupted.

"I am injured, and I need ... "

"Why are you here?"

Grant understood that he was expected to go deeper, and he tried to do that. "In Paraguay, I healed a boy, and afterward I was kidnapped and hung. I think it was punishment. Maybe a lesson. I did many things poorly and caused unnecessary suffering."

"You healed a boy?"

"No, Uncle. It was the ancient ones. The spirits who come dancing. I don't know how or why. I cannot heal anyone."

The old man nodded. "Why are you here?" he asked again.

Grant thought for a long time. This would go on all day until he came to the root of things.

"My Uncle, I spent my life as a journalist. I was a rational man searching for truth. But I have seen things and heard things and sensed things that tell me that … that the rational world I imagined is … it's too small to hold every truth."

Brebeuf nodded, but persisted. "Why are you here, Crow Eyes?"

Grant considered the questions for several minutes. "I am here because I feel the need to reconcile my rational nature with my spiritual being. I am not having much luck."

"None of us are."

"You mean you have the same problem?" Grant had never considered that Brebeuf might not be perfect in his understanding. "You are a fourth degree Midew."

"What does it mean to you that I am a Midew?"

"That you are a medicine man. You practice the ancient arts of healing and storytelling, according to the traditions of the Midewiwin society. And you protect the birchbark scrolls and the history and culture of the Ojibwe people."

"What else?"

"You are of the Bear Clan, the healers and protectors of the Ojibwe."

"What else?"

"Frankly, that you are very secretive. And I don't know why."

"The Midewiwin is a secret society. It has been so for hundreds of years. I learned it in secret from my father. He kept it a secret even from most of his family. Your grandmother was a great Midew. Did she ever tell you?"

"No. I spent every summer with her on the reservation when I was boy. She taught me many things and I would watch her speak to people and make medicines for them. But she never said she was Midew. I learned years after her death from a woman who had studied under her."

"You mean the woman named Deedeens? It means blue jay in the old language."

"Yes," Grant confirmed. "Are all Ojibwe medicine people Midewiwin?" he asked.

"No."

"There are many shamans who claim to be healers and diviners. How many of them are Midewiwin?"

"None, probably."

"How can you tell?"

"Because they promote themselves. They make claims. They collect money for their services." Brebeuf nodded and Grant understood.

"If the spirits are willing to heal you," Brebeuf said, "They will guide you to the ones who can help. Remember how you first found me?"

"I saw you in a dream."

Brebeuf nodded again. "Let us do a story."

"First, tell me about the Midewiwin degrees."

"It is like anything else. It is just levels of experience and ability. It is not formal. The first degree is for those who have finished training on all the herbs and barks and roots that are used in our medicines. The second comes when one also shows the ability to read the spirits of people and understand what is troubling them. Or maybe it comes just because the person has become especially good at the medicines."

"Who decides these things?"

"The Midewiwin members themselves, meeting in secret."

"It is like a democracy?"

"The Ojibwe have always been a democratic people. It has always amazed us that so many others are not."

"What about the third degree?"

"This is awarded rarely, and only to those who can summon the ancients for the purpose of healing. Your grandmother, for example."

"And the fourth?"

"The fourth and highest degree is awarded, I guess you would say, as an honor, after many years as a third degree. Now let's do a story."

"I think I'm too tired. You will want me to think more than I am willing to think."

"Our stories are made simple, for children to learn. They have simple messages that children understand. But they are like onions. You have to peel away the layers. That can be hard work."

"I know."

"Many stories can only be told in their season. But it is winter, the season of stories. It has been so for hundreds of years. Today, let us talk about two characters you mentioned, Wenebojo and Aayaash. Tell me what you know about them."

Grant took a deep breath and began. "Well, Wenebojo is in a lot of stories. He is like a superman. He's sort of half man and half spirit. He's very human in his desires, but he has special powers and he can talk to the animals. He's a trickster. He's always up to something."

"And how is Aayaash different?"

"I don't think he's a spirit at all. He's all human, but he is helped by the spirits. He leads a very hard life. He is abused by his father and betrayed by his people. He goes on a series of adventures, each of which has a separate message. I think the Aayaash stories are older than the others."

"In your chant, you spoke of Aayaash abandoned on an island with no way off. But the Horned Serpent, who is usually bad, offers Aayaash a ride on his back. When they get to shore, the great eagle, who is usually good, kills the serpent. Was that right?"

"No, Uncle."

"The spirits sent you to that far-off place to heal that boy, and then sent you home a cripple. They sent you home with nothing, not even a wife, who might have come back to you if you were not a cripple."

"I probably deserved it."

"If we all got what we deserved, we would be killed as children."

"Then why do you think they sent me back like this?"

"Maybe it was just a joke." Brebeuf cackled for nearly a full minute, paused for a bit and then cackled again. "And that is your lesson for today. You grew up half white, and you confuse Christian thinking with Ojibwe. Christians have a perfect God who knows everything, sees everything and loves everyone.

"We have no such god. Even the Great Mystery, *Gichi Manitou,* does not know the future. And spirits are people who were imperfect in this world and are likely to be imperfect in the next. Some may help you. Others may torment you. All of them have agendas of their own. You cannot trust them."

"You don't much like Christianity."

"It teaches man's dominion over the Earth. What have your Ojibwe stories told you?"

"That we are all equal, every living thing. People, animals, trees … all life."

"There are not two worlds, man's world and the natural world. There is only the one. Turtle island. We have to live together."

"Of course."

"But people are different in some ways. We have a mind. We are both logical and spiritual. We need balance."

"Harmony."

"It is a struggle. If the logical wins out, you will find many questions cannot be answered, and your mind will be limited. If the spiritual wins out, you will lose your curiosity. You will stop even asking the questions, and your mind will be wasted.

"The harmony we seek is not a state of peace. It is a state of balance. And to find that balance is a constant struggle, like a large bird balancing on a wire.

"Accept the spirits in your life, Crow Eyes, but take responsibility for what you do. The spirits will not save you. They will not save the people. Use your mind to do what is right. Remember that it was a spirit who gave Aayaash the flaming arrow, and with it he burned down the world."

"Yes," Grant acknowledged. "I was reading about this stuff the science people call LUCA. Do you know about that?"

"It's the Last Universal Common Ancestor. It lived billions of years ago, in the ocean, and from it all life descended. There were other living things back then, but their lines died out. We all come from LUCA: animals, plants, insects . . . everything that is alive. I feel in my heart this is correct. It fits into my Ojibwe heritage. We are all related. We are a family."

"Germs, too? Viruses?"

"In every family there are problems, Crow Eyes. None are perfect. I know this new disease has caused you to feel bad now about this world. And you have lost faith in your neighbors. In your leaders. Many have acted badly. But to be whole, you must find your love again. Be patient with your brethren. Make peace with the imperfect world around you. It is the only family you have."

EIGHT

RADISSON AND Undersheriff Jim Beeksma and two deputies walked in a line, four abreast, probing the snow with long shafts of rebar.

The two dogs just sprawled out in the snow, showing little interest in the activities. They were trained to smell cadavers, but having smelled nothing, they had decided to take the day off.

Beeksma was, as usual, in a testy mood. "Ho-lee-cow," he snarled. "I don't even know what we're feeling for. If that old man has been laying under this snow for two weeks, he's frozen hard. You hit him and it's going to feel the same as hitting the ground."

"Maybe," Radisson conceded.

"I can't breathe," Beeksma added. "We shouldn't be out here working in this bad air. All this crap must be coming from those forest fires in Minnesota."

"Probably."

"It can't all be coming from California and Colorado."

"It's worse in Australia."

"Jeez, it's thick enough to chew. Can I take off this damn Covid mask?"

"No."

"I can't breathe. And the dogs aren't going to smell a frozen cadaver. Not in all this smoke."

"My dog could smell it," one deputy countered. "He could smell the odor from before the body froze. Hell, he can smell a body in six feet of water."

"Well then, there's nothing here to smell. This is foolish. Let's call it a day."

Weegwasi's land consisted of four adjoining forty-acre parcels on the Raspberry River. His cabin was near the middle of his property, surrounded by hardwoods of every variety, mostly aspen, pin oak and maple. Some very tall white pine were mixed in, and a few red pine and spruce. To the north, toward Lake Superior, the property dropped into a frozen marsh where there were many larch trees, all bare now, having dropped their needles.

The long trail from the road to the house was just a narrow lane. When Radisson drove in, the silence had been the first thing he noticed. The little cabin was so far off the road that ran down from Old Highway K, there was no traffic noise of any kind. It was perfect wilderness, about two miles south of the wild shore of Lake Superior.

When the men had finished walking two concentric circles around the cabin, Radisson ordered a halt and went to talk to an elderly neighbor man and his wife who had come to watch, clinging to each other for support, shivering in the cold and looking downcast.

"He was a wonderful old fella," Mr. Johansen said.

"Wonderful," Mrs. Johansen repeated.

"Always so polite and nice. A wonderful neighbor."

"Polite," she repeated.

"I say neighbor, but hell, we live probably two miles from here. Maybe three. But out here, that's what we call a neighbor. There aren't many homes, so we keep track of each other. We have to. When you help someone, you get help back when you need it."

"You get help," she said.

"Charlie was a little shy. He spoke funny. I don't think he could pronounce the "t-h" sound. He would say 'dis' and 'dat.' Things like that. I think people thought he was a little simple, but he wasn't. He was smart. And hardworking."

"Hardworking," she nodded.

"He would cut down trees with an axe. Who does that anymore? Used them for his baskets. Sold firewood, too."

Radisson was studying a plat book and scratching his head. "I can't tell what is private land and what is public."

"It's a patchwork," Johansen said. "Federal land all along the lake except for some state land. Then there's the tribal land. The county owns all that timber across the road. There are a bunch of forty-acre private parcels, but several of them are held in trust for the tribe or the state government. Timber companies own a lot of the rest. There probably aren't twenty of us who live out here, and most of us don't have electricity."

"A generator," she said.

"When is the last time you saw Mr. Weegwasi?" Radisson wanted to know.

"I don't know, maybe three weeks ago." He looked at Mrs. Johansen.

"Three weeks ago," she confirmed. "About that."

"Did he seem okay?"

"Just like always."

"Did he seem confused at all? Disoriented? Maybe repeat things he'd already said?"

"Just like always. I didn't notice anything."

"Did he say if he was going anywhere, a visit maybe? Relatives?"

"I don't think he ever went anywhere. He has a grandson who comes to see him. I don't think he has any other family. I know a nurse or a social worker of some kind from Red Cliff would come out to check on him. The tribe is pretty good about keeping track of their folks."

"Did he have any enemies that you know of? Anyone who would want to hurt him?"

"Charlie? Are you kidding? Almost nobody even knows him, and he has never said an ill word about anyone in his life."

"Just the spirits," she said.

Mr. Johansen laughed. "Yeah, old Charlie was a superstitious guy. I suppose it was the way he was brought up. He saw evil spirits in everything. Had a bunch of words for them."

"*Bagwajiwinii?*"

"Yeah, that's one." Johansen was impressed Radisson would know an *Anishinaabe* spirit word. "Then there was another one he talked about last time we were here. I can't think what it was." He looked at his wife.

"I can't think of it," she said.

"He acted like he was genuinely scared. But that wasn't so unusual."

The other men had wandered off to search through the woodshed and smokehouse. Beeksma had gone into the cabin to sit down, out of the smoke. One of the deputies was on his knees at the side of the cabin, right under the window. He hollered out. "Sheriff, I think you should look at this."

Radisson excused himself and went back to the cabin.

"You getting anything?" the deputy asked.

"His neighbors talk about him in the past tense, like he's dead for sure. It's a bit suspicious. But I don't know."

"Well look at this." The deputy pulled away a small piece of canvas and underneath it was what looked like two tracks in the snow. The back of the foot looked human, but was huge, maybe four times the size of a normal man. The front had claws, or toes like a bird.

"What the hell?"

"I saw this piece of canvas sticking up. It had about a foot of snow on it. When I pulled it up, the snow came with it and underneath were these tracks."

"It looks like someone covered the tracks to protect them from the snow."

"What do you make of that?"

"Well, I don't know, deputy. What am I supposed to make of it, for God's sake?"

"This is creepy. Whatever made these tracks was standing right here, looking in this window."

"Sheriff," Mr. Johansen shouted. "I just thought of that word."

NINE

“WHAT THE hell is a *wiindigoog*?” Radisson roared.

Sam Grant, who had thus far gotten nothing but telemarketer calls and was already sorry he had found his phone, was doubly sorry now. “Lewis, you’re shouting,” he said calmly into the phone.

“Well, every time I get involved in one of these reservation cases, I regret it. Every time. I swear, the next time some old man up here disappears, I’m just gonna send flowers to his family.”

“Did you find anything?”

“Not what I was looking for.”

“No sign of Mr. Weegwasi?”

“Like he vanished into air. What I found were the tracks of something that walks around in the snow barefooted. It looks like the track of a human, but he is, oh, probably fifteen feet tall. Has toes like a bird. Sound like one of your friends?”

“Doesn’t ring a bell.”

“He stands next to Weegwasi’s window so he can look in.”

“A peeping giant. You don’t see a lot of them.”

"Charlie's neighbor says the old man was complaining about some *wiindigoog*. Am I saying that right?"

"Close enough. Does he think Charlie turned into a *wiindigoog*?"

"I don't know. Do you old Indians do things like that? They think he was scared."

"Where did the tracks go?"

"I don't know. They are not fresh. They are under several days of snow. But someone threw a piece of canvas over some of them to protect them."

"Really?"

"What is a *wiindigoog*?"

"It's complicated," Grant explained. "The word gets used a lot and the meaning shifts. A *wiindigoog* can be just a greedy and thoughtless person who consumes the earth's resources and destroys the environment. Traditionally, as Charlie would understand the word, a *wiindigoog* is a man whose spirit has turned evil, maybe through greed and corruption, maybe as a result of eating human flesh. In any case, he turns into a huge, malevolent creature who hunts people and eats them."

"Does he have toes like a bird?"

"There is no one description. He could be anything. But he is usually very tall and very thin, with long arms and legs. And horns."

"Just a minute, Sam."

Radisson slid from his truck and pulled his Glock. The other deputies and the neighbors had all left. The sheriff had stayed behind to take pictures of the tracks and the inside of the cabin, then he had put crime scene tape around the door. Now he was alone in all that quiet, and he was sure he had heard something.

He looked every direction, and when he turned one way there was a cracking sound in the woods behind him. He spun that way and flipped off the safety.

The wind rushed through the treetops. Somewhere a long way off a crow called. It was very cold and a tree suddenly burst, going off like a rifle shot.

"I know someone or something is around here," he whispered into the phone.

"You're just jittery. The smoke and the epidemic. We are all a little out of sorts."

"Sam, I was twenty years in the army. I know when there's something around. Hold on. I'm going to put you on speaker and put the phone down."

From his truck, Radisson pulled out a little case. Without taking his eyes off the woods around him, he extracted the thermal imaging scope inside. It was designed to work in the dark, but it was smoky enough and cold enough that anything warm out there would jump right out.

He panned the scope around the whole perimeter. Even the bushes and trees showed gradients of color, being warmer than the snow. When he had looked everywhere, he went back to one spot that was quite bright. Just a little spot. Maybe a bird, he thought.

He put the scope away and took out his binoculars. As he focused in on the spot, he could see a yellow eye. It was looking right at him. A little yellow eye.

He zoomed back a little and he could see that around the eye was half the head of a wolf. It was standing behind a tree, and what was visible was just one ear, one eye and half of a very black nose. It stood motionless. The eye never blinked.

"It's just a wolf," Radisson said.

"There is never just one wolf," Grant responded. "Hold on."

Radisson zoomed back some more and scanned farther around. There was a second wolf, fully exposed, facing him, motionless in the snow. It was twenty yards behind the first wolf, but it took a slow step forward, then another. The snow was mostly new and not strong enough to support the weight of the animal. But the wolf's legs were surprisingly long, and though snow came up to its belly, it stepped along with perfect grace, making no sound at all.

"I see another one," Radisson whispered. "How many more will there be?"

"Some. Usually."

He turned all the way around, scanning behind, not wanting to feel surrounded. "I don't see any others."

"Probably it's the alpha pair out hunting on their own. They will do that. How do they look?"

"Big. Healthy. But they must be hungry. They can't chase down a deer in this deep snow."

"They go two weeks between meals. Longer if they have to."

Radisson jumped when a loaf of snow fell from a pine limb and landed right behind.

"Listen to me, Sam. I am about a million miles from nowhere. There is not a human sound around. The wind is whistling, and the smoke is thick as fog. The old man who lives here is missing. I got hungry wolves looking at me like I'm lunch. And some Indian Big Bird is running around barefoot making tracks the size of a hubcap. I am about as creeped out as I can be."

"Imagine how Weegwasi might have felt."

"You think he took off?"

"I don't know. But if you wanted to tell people what was happening, and you couldn't write, what would you do?"

Radisson thought. "I'd protect those tracks so people would find them and know. You think those tracks are real?"

"I bet Weegwasi thought they were real. He should know."

"What do we do?"

"I don't know, Lewis. We're not making any progress. If that old man is still alive, in weather like this, he won't last long. If you were afraid and couldn't drive, where would you go? Where's the nearest house? Or the nearest phone?"

"Miles from here. The closest would be the Johansens, and they haven't seen him. There's no other place. You could never walk out of here in this weather."

Grant sucked in air and tried to think what to do. When he thought of it, he tried to think of something else, but couldn't.

"Well, Lewis, I guess we're going to have to go on a *wiindigoog* hunt."

"*You're* going to have to go on a w*iindigoog* hunt, my long-haired friend. You and your medicine bag and your knee-high moccasins and your bad leg. Me, I think I'll take a little vacation to Florida."

"Do you mind if I go up there to his cabin tomorrow? I was going to Red Cliff anyway."

"You won't last ten minutes in this spook hole, Mr. Shaman. I'm white as a ghost and I don't even believe in this Indian crap."

"Ten minutes may be all I need."

"Listen, if you're going to Red Cliff, the neighbors say there is a tribal social worker who visits here often."

"I'll check that out."

An owl swooped right past Radisson's head and landed on a nearby limb. The bird turned its head all the way around and just stared at the sheriff. Radisson turned to check back on the wolves. The first one was still motionless behind the tree. The second was ten yards closer now, and still coming.

"I'm getting the hell out of here," he said.

TEN

HENRY GOKEE, as always, was in the office of the Red Cliff Band of the Lake Superior Chippewa. Chairperson of the nine-member council, he took his job seriously, but his many years of responsibility had taken a toll.

"I'll tell you the truth," he said, rummaging through a tall metal file cabinet. "I wouldn't do this for anyone else, Sam. I don't have the time."

"I appreciate it, Henry," Grant said.

"I want to do what I can for old man Weegwasi. He is a great artist. But look at my desk."

Sam did, and what he saw were piles of papers and files, uneven stacks tottering on the edge, defying gravity. "Goodness," Sam said.

"That damned lake is about to swallow us," Gokee growled. "Old *Gitche Gumee*, the big shining sea. She has taken all she can take and she's coming to get us, Sam."

"Flooding?"

"Flooding. Soaked utility lines. Water right up to some of the roads. Water clear over some driveways. Don't know what we're going to do with the Marina next spring. The beaches are gone. The wharfs are about under water. Hell, it's the same all up and down the south shore. Port Wing, Herbster, Cornucopia. You got break walls in Port Wing that are damn near submerged. The herring shed in Sand Point is gone. The ice is dangerous because the water level keeps changing."

"It's the same everywhere," Grant said. "Maybe it's because the arctic ice is melting."

"The ice is melting, but you know what those government scientists tell us? They say the problem is there is too much ice on Lake Superior."

"Too much?"

"Too much. They say the polar ice cap floats, so it won't raise the water level as it melts. But all the ice in Superior is inhibiting evaporation and causing the lake to rise."

"Good Lord."

Gokee looked at Sam directly for the first time and curled his lip into a snarl. "But I know what the problem really is. Do you want to hear it?"

"Sure."

"The problem is, there's more water going into the lake than coming out. How about that?"

"Sounds right to me."

"It's as simple as that. All that water has to go somewhere, so it is going into rain and snow and humidity and dew and what-have-you, all over the watershed. And its running into Lake Superior faster than it can run out."

"Not likely to stop."

"Not gonna stop, and those piles on my desk are gonna get higher and higher, just like the lake. I'm either going to drown in water or drown in paper."

"I'm sorry, Henry."

"And now we got a damn plane crash. Two people dead and enough feds running around to start a war. I think every letter of the alphabet is represented out there, except maybe five or six. And we'll have them as soon as the government opens a bureau called the XYZ."

"Drug smugglers?"

"Probably. One was wearing clothes made in Russia."

"Russian Mafia?"

"Mafias, cartels, what have you. Everyone thinks reservations are soft spots in law enforcement. What they don't know is that if they come here, they're all likely to drown. One of these days I'm just going to walk out of this place. Tear off this damn mask. Find myself a nice high hill with a tall house. A place above the water and the smoke. Then I'm just going to sit down on the porch and watch the show."

The Red Cliff reservation has more than twenty miles of undeveloped Lake Superior shoreline, with some of the most awe-inspiring vistas in the world, looking out over the rocky Apostle Islands. But it's a surprisingly small place, just under 15,000 acres. It is really just a narrow band of land that follows along the lakeshore. Half the 5,000 enrolled members live off the reservation in nearby towns or, like Charlie Weegwasi, in the wild land near the reservation.

"Here it is," Henry said, pulling a file from the cabinet. "I can't let you look at it. It's a private document. But I think I can tell you what you need to know." He sat down and read for a few minutes. "Yup. It's like you thought. He has 160 acres in four parcels, and, upon his death, they will pass into the custody of the Tribal Council, along with easements of record and etcetera. Let's see. There's one provision. A man named James Birch is entitled to use the house and maintain and use the outbuildings for as long as he lives. You know this James Birch?"

"That's Charlie's grandson."

"The one who reported him missing?"

"Yes."

"Huh. He changed his name."

"I guess he did. Or his dad, maybe."

"Weegwasi means birchbark."

"Uh-huh."

"He just kept a little of the name and made it white.

"Uh-huh."

"Must be a proud Ojibwe, huh? Why are you writing all this down? I've never seen you take notes."

"Does it bother you?"

"I'd feel better if I knew why you were doing it."

"No, you would feel worse."

"Try me."

"I'm writing it down because, by tomorrow, I probably won't remember a thing you said."

"Oh … I'm sorry, Sam.… You were right. I feel worse. Anyway, you got what you needed. Nobody stands to gain anything from his death, at least not his land."

"Henry, there is a tribal nurse or social worker who has been visiting Charlie. Do you know who that might be?"

"I got 300 employees, Sam. Ask at the Family and Human Services building."

"With your permission, I will do that."

"Oh hell, you'd do it without my permission."

Grant smiled. "There is always a way."

"You are being uncommonly polite today. You usually raise hell."

"You are being uncommonly cooperative, Henry. I don't have to raise hell."

"We're too old to keep fighting it out, Sam. You got brain problems and can hardly walk, and you got one eye closed. And I'm just worn out. Just plain worn out."

"Do you have anyone working on the plane crash?"

"Oh hell, no. It's reserved for people from out of state. I don't even think the sheriff has been there."

"He hasn't. It's tribal land."

"We got a new patrolman, a vet we sent to evidence school. I think he's been there, after everyone else left. I doubt he learned anything."

"Would you mind if I talk to him?"

"Jacob Dewberry. He grew up at Lac Court Oreilles. Two tours in Afghanistan, but he still looks about sixteen. Smart though. Real smart."

ELEVEN

AGNES DEPERRY grew up in Red Cliff, graduated from Bayfield High School, did some college in Superior, and had been a tribal social worker for thirty years. She knew everything that happened on or near the reservation, and who made it happen, and usually why.

She knew all about Sam Grant, knew he had spent years as a big city reporter and more years as a correspondent in the Middle East, Horn of Africa and the Balkans. She knew about his run-ins with Standing Bear and the Bear Clan. Knew about his many clashes over the years with Henry Gokee. Knew about Sam's grandmother, his daughter's murder in Milwaukee, his failed marriage, and his dalliances with Jennifer Deedeens and Bette Smallwood.

She even knew about his trips to Paraguay, knew he had been kidnapped there and hung and nearly killed. She knew he had gone there to withdraw money. She had heard it said that Grant had a fortune stashed away in banks all over the world, money he had sort of inherited from a hired killer. Or something like that.

She did not know he would look this bad.

"*Boozhoo,*" she said, using the traditional Ojibwe greeting. And Grant knew he was in for a test. She insisted on conducting this interview in *Anishinaabemowin,* the Ojibwe traditional language. She said there were still 50,000 native speakers in North America, that all Red Cliff children were now being given emersion classes, and it was the least they could do, as senior member of the band, to speak it themselves.

Grant, who spoke five other languages, struggled with this one. It was mostly verbs, and you created sentences through slight manipulations of the verb and inflexions of the voice. Very different words sounded almost exactly the same. And he had suspicions that much of the language was not even old.

The Ojibwe had always been open to other cultures and beliefs, and he thought they had assimilated lots of words, too. Indeed, Boozhoo sounds very much like *Bonjour,* the greeting they would have heard from the French trappers and the French Jesuit priests who first penetrated their Great Lakes world.

Probably the Ojibwe back then didn't have a word for hello, like they didn't have a word for please, and just adopted one. Both are useless words, appended to white languages to express politeness in white societies that were, otherwise, scarcely polite at all.

Why would one say please in a native culture wherein sharing everything - from food to labor - was expected? There was no need for a word to essentially beg for a gift that was expected, always given freely and required by custom.

Grant played along as best as he could, admitting that he failed to see how his stumbling use of *Anishnaabemowin* befitted any children.

The test finally ended and Grant didn't know how he had done. He had gotten no useful information about Charlie Weegwasi, except that Charlie spoke only his native language when she visited, and wasn't very good with English. She loved the man, respected his considerable skill and artistry, but otherwise hated going to his home because, visibly overweight, she was uncomfortable in a place so wild and rude.

After that she sat for a long time not saying anything, she behind her mask and Sam behind his, neither able to read anything into expressions they could not see. Sam said nothing either. This was another test. Ojibwe, unlike white people, are comfortable with long pauses and periods of silence.

Finally, she looked him over, top to bottom, and said, "Physician, heal thyself."

"I'm sorry, ma'am?"

"I have heard that you are a great healer, a medicine man, a Midew of great power. Have you looked into a mirror?"

"Perhaps the people you listen to are prone to exaggeration," he said. But then he was suddenly very offended, something that didn't happen much. It was one thing to make fun of him, but it was quite another to scoff at the Midewiwin. It was against custom. The Mede had been, for thousands of years, the keepers of the tribal culture, the stories, the herbal cures, the ceremonies and the songs. They were the keepers of the sacred birchbark scrolls containing a set of hieroglyphs that hovered on the edge of being a rudimentary written language, something no other native culture had ever produced. It was the life's work of his grandmother, a third degree Midew, and Mr. Brebeuf, a fourth degree.

"Or perhaps I can heal myself," he said icily. "And choose not to."

She leaned forward. "Why would anyone choose not to heal himself?"

"Perhaps because what you see is what I deserve."

"Have you been a bad boy?"

"I have been too arrogant, almost my whole life. How about you?"

Agnes looked down and shuffled some papers. She swallowed, then swallowed again.

"I'm sorry," she said. "With me, it is something new. Maybe I need to retire."

"Mrs. Deperry, do you know how Mr. Weegwasi handles his money? He is illiterate."

"I have his checkbook," she said. "I've been writing his checks for years. At least fifteen. So do you want to audit me?"

"Isn't that an unusual arrangement for a social worker?"

"Not really." She smiled. "It's not quite what you think. His grandson and I each have a checkbook and we both get monthly statements. It's like dual control. We can keep track of each other."

"If I may ask, how much money are we talking about?"

"Well, in the old days, at powwow, Charlie would make $100,000 or more. Now, it's half that. Of course, it has to last all year, buy his food and medicine and pay for his expenses. He used to make all his dyes, but lately he's been buying some. He's never held a real job, so he doesn't get any social security, but he's comfortable."

"He must have saved a good deal by now."

"About five years ago he started contributing to the tribal food bank. It has drained his savings. He has maybe $20,000 left."

"How about Mr. Birch, his grandson? Does he write many checks?"

"Almost none. He will buy a tool or something now and then for his grandfather. I think mostly he spends his own money."

"Tell me about him."

"You haven't met him? He lives in Rice Lake."

"I'm going Friday."

"Well, I don't know. He's a real nice guy. Easy going. Maybe forty, which should tell you how old Charlie is."

"Yes."

"He visits every two weeks, almost like clockwork. That way Charlie can know when he's coming and save up jobs for him. Charlie doesn't have a phone."

"He helps?"

"Oh God, yeah. Charlie can't move those big logs by himself. He counts on James for help with all the heavy work. I think it very impressive that James is so devoted to him. He has plenty to do already, I'm sure. He owns a bunch of restaurants. He is quite well-to-do."

"Really?"

"I know he would like to put Charlie into a facility, and I understand why. But I can't see that ever happening."

"Do they argue?"

"Mr. Grant, I don't know what they do. I think they love each other. I can tell you James calls me every day, frantic for information. He is so worried."

"Where do you stand on a facility?"

"The day Charlie goes into a home will be the day he produces his last basket. It would be a terrible loss."

"He must not be doing many baskets anymore."

"More than you think."

"The sheriff says there aren't any at his house."

"There aren't ever any baskets at his house. I've never seen one. He must keep them somewhere else."

"For the life of me, I can't see any motive for anyone to hurt him. He must have just run off. Maybe he fell in the snow and couldn't get up. Maybe he became disoriented and got lost." Agnes Deperry just sat like a stone. "I take it you don't agree."

"Mr. Grant, Charlie Weegwasi is well over 80, but he gets around better than you. He is a little man and very flexible. He still bounces up and down. He has lived in the wilderness all his life. He knows what he can do and what he can't."

"What do think happened to him?"

"He may have gone somewhere we don't know about, to a friend's maybe, someone he's never talked about. He is not real open about certain things."

"If he got scared, he might do that. Did he ever talk to you about spirits? *Wiindigoog,* things like that?"

"Oh, let's see," she chuckled. "Maybe every day. Charlie thinks spirits are behind everything, including his baskets. Good spirits and bad spirits. When he gets an idea for a really wonderful basket, he thinks it came from a spirit."

"Did he ever seem to be afraid of a spirit?"

"Every day."

"Huh." Grant sighed. "It's hard to know where to go with this. Can you remember any name he ever talked about? A buyer. A supplier. A helper. Someone who might be that secret friend?"

She shook her head and thought. "This is pretty far out," she said.

"That's okay."

"My husband does construction, and he says a rich guy who has a big home down by the lake came around looking for someone with a bulldozer and grader who could put in a road for him. No, it's a crazy idea."

"What?"

"Well, the guy said he was trying to make a new way into his house because it was so far out of his way to go through the reservation, and the road was about to flood."

"There's a lot of that going on."

"My husband asked me if Charlie had mentioned that, because when he looked at a map, the only possible shortcut would be to come in by Old Highway K, through Charlie's land."

"Had Charlie ever mentioned that?"

"No."

"I would think if he were going sell a piece of his land, he would tell you."

"Without doubt. But he would never sell that land. Any of it. It has the only sweet grass around that I know of. It has black ash for his baskets and right tree roots for the lashings. It has iron deposits and clays and barks for dye."

"Suppose someone just wanted to buy it, or put a road through it, and Charlie objected. Would he have told you about that?"

"Almost certainly."

Grant leaned back into his chair. "It's probably nothing, but I'd like that man's name."

"I'll get it from my husband."

"If you would, please call Bayfield County Sheriff Lewis Radisson and tell him what you told me. I probably wouldn't remember the name if you gave it to me."

"Of course. And I'm sorry if I said something improper about the Midewiwin. I know they are an important part of our heritage. As I recall, your grandmother was one. I'm sure there are others, but I don't know who they are."

"It is a secret society. You are not supposed to know. Mrs. Deperry, what do you think about Charlie Weegwasi? You know him as well as anyone. Do you think Charlie is gone? Or is he someday just going to walk right back into his house and make a basket?"

"It's one or the other," she nodded. "I'd say the odds are about even right now. But as time passes, the odds change. And for the worse."

TWELVE

THE SMOKE was thicker and darker in the forest than on the roads. The canopy of trees seemed to hold it in, and it blew in small clouds along the ground. As soon as Grant turned off Highway K, he started coughing.

The trail in had been broken by several sheriff's vehicles, but his truck still wanted to slide sideways.

Driving with one hand and one eye and occasional waves of nausea, Grant had done okay until then. He slid to a stop and wondered if he should go on. But he had made it down Mr. Brebeuf's track, so he could make it down Mr. Weegwasi's.

He was exhausted by the time he reached the old cabin, and when he opened his truck door, wolves scattered in every direction. At least six, he decided. But probably seven. Could have been more he didn't see. He got back in and closed the door and rested.

About an acre of land had been largely cleared around the cabin, but old-growth white pine, 200 feet tall, were scattered about. They were five or six feet in diameter, and their tops so high—and so covered in snow—that they seemed to fade out against the smoke and the low sky. The quiet was deafening, even for Grant, who had just spent two weeks at his uncle's cabin.

Beyond the clearing was dense forest, parts of it made denser by thick stands of small aspen growing just inches apart. Several trails webbed out from the clearing into the woods. Since Radisson had come and left the day before, it had stopped snowing, and the pristine white had become deeply tracked by deer and coyotes and wolves. The elongated feet of rabbits had bounded across the top of the snow, and crows had etched trails of their own. An owl had landed in one spot, and with its wings had graded a circle six feet across. In the middle something had met its end. Grant couldn't tell what. Maybe a rabbit or some other rodent. Maybe a bird. The owl had carried it away, leaving only drops of blood.

Feeling better, he stepped out again and took snowshoes from the truck bed. He didn't know exactly how to hunt a *wiindigoog*, but he didn't think it would take long.

He did one circle around the cabin in the snowshoes, trying to read its recent history. He could see where the deputies had probed with polls. The door had been crosshatched with crime scene tape. The canvas still covered the tracks by the window. The place had been otherwise undisturbed. That seemed odd.

Weegwasi had a grandson, had neighbors, had a tribal clan and a social worker friend. Didn't anybody even try to look for him? Or, like the sheriff, had they all been discouraged by the deep snow and despairing of the outcome?

Grant clunked awkwardly onto the porch and looked in the unlocked door. But he didn't go in. He saw the rifle and the gun in a rack. He saw the empty peg on a coatrack. And he found the nails outside, next to the door, where snowshoes would have hung.

There was a smokehouse and shed behind the cabin. The smokehouse had been unused since early fall. The shed contained, on stretchers, the pelts of a skunk, a beaver and three weasels. There was also the hindquarter of a deer, a big one, safely frozen. It should last until spring. The hide had been recently stripped away and left on the floor in a frozen heap.

Nearby was a large lean-to woodshed holding at least five cords, most of it popple, sawed into wheels and neatly split. Lots of old-timers didn't burn popple, but it's a good, clean-burning firewood if you keep it dry. Piles of bark from a paper birch were nearby, for starter.

A short-tail weasel stood warily on the cords and looked at Grant. A mottled gray, it was still in the process of turning pure white, with a black-tipped tail. It would soon be a beautiful ermine.

"It's up to you, of course," Grant told the weasel, "but if I were you, I'd step carefully around here. There are three more just like you in the shed, and they each took one step too many." The animal hurried off over the snow and into the bushes. Must be nice, Grant thought, to become an ermine. Grant would always be a weasel.

On the other side of the cabin, a dark area caught his attention. When he reached it, he found a deer carcass frozen in the snow and largely stripped clean. That's why the wolves had been here. And the many tracks proved foxes and coyotes and crows had feasted, as well. So had the weasel, and a wolverine and probably a fisher. Maybe two.

Even a little chipmunk had emerged for a mid-winter snack. Grant did a deep knee bend and touched the little chipper track. "Tourists think you're a cute little pet," Grant whispered. "They feed you potato chips. If they could look into your heart, they would see a killer, a hunter of mice, part carnivore, always in search of an easy meal."

Grant pulled up the carcass. It was a large doe, with a hindquarter missing. Underneath was a plastic sled with a towrope. He rose again and realized the dizzy thing was suddenly much better. He could look down without falling over. At least if he were careful. The cold and the wild were rejuvenating him, like they always had. He wasn't ready to celebrate, but he was ready to get a good look at those tracks by the window.

He pulled the canvas away and was happy to see the tracks had not been molested. But there was enough snow in them that the back part that had looked human to Radisson was now too indistinct to tell. The toe marks were clear, but they didn't look like any bird Grant knew, and he knew them all. Maybe *wiindigoog* were a different kind of bird ... or half-bird.

Something bothered him about the tracks, and after he thought for a minute, he knew. He retrieved a plastic snow shovel from the porch and dug a hole right next to one track, all the way down to the ground. He got on his knees and studied the profile of the snow, testing its texture at different levels. Then he called Radisson.

"What kind of fifteen-foot monster leaves a track six inches deep in eighteen inches of soft snow?"

"I don't know," Radisson said. "I take it you're at Weegwasi's place."

"How much do you figure a fifteen-foot man-bird would weigh?"

"I hadn't thought of that," Lewis admitted. "Offhand, I'd say he was on snowshoes."

"Uh-huh."

"Those tracks are about the size of small bear-paw snowshoes."

"Uh-huh."

"It wouldn't be hard to doctor up a snowshoe on the bottom to look like that."

"Some rubber or silicone. And some toes made of welded steel."

"Yeah, but why on earth?"

"I don't know, Lewis. But somebody didn't just walk in and kill Charlie. They scared the crap out of him. Why they did that, I don't know. What happened after that, I don't know. But for sure it was planned. It was a crime, and I am now worried as hell about Charlie."

"It could be the perfect murder. If someone scared him so badly he went running off into the snow, and died, there would be absolutely no evidence."

"Unless you can find the doctored snowshoes."

"Even so, the snowshoes wouldn't be illegal. You couldn't prove anything. The whole crime scene is going to melt in a few months. Did you find anything else?"

"Charlie shot a big doe recently and took a quarter. The rest he left as an offering for *ma'iingan,* the wolves. That's why they hang around here. He probably does that quite a bit."

"Why on earth? A wolf habituated to humans is extremely dangerous."

"It's an Ojibwe thing. An old story. Wenebojo, the man, and *ma'iingan,* the wolf, were brothers and companions. They kept each other company, and together they toured the earth, which we call Turtle Island. They named all the animals. Eventually the man and the wolf had to go their own ways, but people and wolves would remain forever intertwined as brothers and sisters, and whatever happened to one would happen to the other."

"I think I understand."

"That turned out to be true," Grant said. "Wolves were almost wiped out, and so were the Ojibwe. Charlie gave a lot of money to the food bank. He made beautiful baskets for people. He lived by himself, but he did what he could for others. I think Charlie would see that caring for the wolves was a way of caring for the future of his people."

"You are starting to talk about him in the past tense," Radisson observed.

"I'm not sure, Lewis. I'm really not. But it doesn't look good."

"A woman you talked to in Red Cliff called and gave me the name and number of a man who has a big house somewhere north of Weegwasi. What is her name? Agnew Defoe? Something like that.

"I don't remember."

"Well, that figures. Anyway, I'm checking it out. I called the guy and got no answer so I'm driving up there right now. What are you going to do?"

"I think I'll look around a little more, then go on home. I'm pretty tired."

"Well, what you've done is helpful, Sam. Thank you. Don't feed the wolves, if you know what I mean."

THIRTEEN

THE WOLVES were nowhere in sight, but Grant could feel their eyes on him. Their tracks were everywhere around the cabin, and leading off toward the trails into the woods. One trail in particular was heavily used.

"*Boozhoo*, my brothers," he called out. "It is a good day."

Grant stood up and put his phone away. He pulled the wool cap down over his ears and clapped his gloves together. It was clear but cold. He took a deep breath and the moisture in his nostrils froze. What could he do, in his condition? He wanted to search, but it seemed impossible. Shuffling along in snowshoes is a demanding activity, even for a healthy man.

His anger rose. Why on earth had nobody even tried to find Charlie Weegwasi? How could his grandson sit at his home in Rice Lake, knowing his grandad was missing, and not even try? How is it that Agnes Deperry never organized a search, when the tribe's young men would have been eager to help?

Was it possible that the people who knew Weegwasi best knew a search was useless, knew he was beyond their help? And how did they know that?

Grant walked as best he could toward the edge of the clearing, and in his mind he ran a movie of what he knew so far. In his movie, Charlie Weegwasi is sitting quietly by his stove when someone or something peers into his cabin window, maybe bangs on the glass.

Charlie looks up and sees ... what? Something. A *wiindigoog*. Or a man in a mask. The kind of mask you would make if you had made snowshoes that looked like the feet of a man-bird.

For a minute, Charlie freezes in terror. Then he dashes wildly out his door. All around are the giant tracks of a *wiindigoog*. The old man is already susceptible to spirit stories, but now he is beyond reason. He runs off into the woods as fast as he can. Maybe the *wiindigoog* is chasing him. He is old and cannot run fast. In the deep snow, he cannot run at all. He can only wallow on, pushing through new snow up to his hips.

Grant closed his eyes and tried to feel his grandmother's calming presence. The thought of her always carried him into a deeper place and brought clarity to his mind. Intuition, maybe. Some way he had of knowing things he could not logically know, but somehow did.

He rewound the movie and started again. Charlie is still terrified, but he grabs a heavy winter coat off the peg before he goes out. He stops outside, on the porch, and puts on his snowshoes.

Grant shakes his head. No, not possible in his state of mind. Charlie grabs the snowshoes off the nails on the porch and runs off into the woods carrying them. No. First he covers the tracks with a piece of canvas to preserve them. Maybe he isn't that scared, but he wants to get away from the house and the bird prints.

"Then what?"

Grant had reached the edge of the clearing to where the main trail begins, the one most heavily tracked by the wolves. He had reached it without ever really thinking about it, so the pain in his left leg had hardly been noticed. Maybe he could go on for a little way.

He looked up the trail and saw that it was little more than a tunnel through the thick grove of small aspen and brush. The sun slipped behind a cloud and everything darkened. In the distance, a wolf howled.

Grant thought of Weegwasi's rifle on the wall, but it was a hundred yards away and beyond his ability. If he were going to search, he would have to go on now, and waste no additional effort. How far could he go?

He shuffled into the tunnel and thought of the story of the muskrat. Of all those who could have been here, he thought, he was certainly the least qualified.

"My brothers the wolves," he shouted. "Do you mind if I walk with you today? Will you permit me here? I mean no harm. I am looking for the old man who hunts with you, and is now gone. Can you help me?"

The end of the tunnel opened into a pine and spruce forest where there was not so much snow because the canopy had caught it on the way down. Though it was easier to walk, his legs were hurting and the cold was making him stiff. He thought of turning back, but something told him to go on, and Grant always listened to that little voice inside.

Suddenly aware of movement off to one side, he looked in time to see two wolves scamper into hiding in some heavy brush. He turned to his right and there were two more, bounding through deeper snow, going on ahead. He stopped and watched them move away until they disappeared into the trees. They did not seem to notice him, but he was sure they had.

If they were hunting him, he knew that some of the wolves would try to chase him toward other wolves waiting ahead. It was their instinct to work in relays, although a single wolf could have easily felled Sam Grant.

He looked for something that might give him an advantage: A big stick. A tree he could climb. Someplace he could protect his back and face.

Of course. It was all clear now. If Charlie had been running through this shallower snow, it would have inflamed the wolves. Nature had wired them to pursue anything that fled. He looked around with new hope, and he instantly saw it, another fifty yards ahead.

It was a huge white pine whose trunk had long ago divided into two trees. The twin trunks formed a wall of wood more than ten feet across, arcing a little to create a semicircle around a spot of ground that had been trampled all the way down to the heavy layer of brown needles underneath.

When he reached the spot, he turned his back to the tree to see what Charlie would have seen. He was protected on three sides, but how would that save him?

It didn't take more than a minute standing like that before Grant saw the print in the snow. A moccasin print. And then he saw the others. And all around them big spots of blood.

FOURTEEN

DOUGLASS KINCAID was not the sort of man you expected to find in Bayfield County, population 15,000, 88 percent white, 10 percent Indian, per capita income $31,000.

Sheriff Radisson looked at Kincaid's house and figured that $31,000 might cover a monthly mortgage payment. Or maybe just a utility bill.

Kincaid was into pharmaceuticals, the high-tech kind. He had bought out a company in Missoula, Montana that had developed a kind of circuit board that could be made on a 3-D printer. It used chemicals rather than electronic parts. According to the internet, the most sophisticated chemical reactions could be made and tested in minute amounts using these circuit boards. It was expected to speed the development of new pharmaceuticals.

But the stories were all six or seven years old. There was nothing new that Radisson's chief clerk and wife, Jackie Beeksma, could find.

What Sheriff Radisson could tell was that Kincaid was a big game hunter who brought home enough trophies from Africa to clutter the walls of the only room the sheriff could see into.

His enormous house—a lodge, really—was surrounded on three sides by Red Cliff tribal land and the Apostles Islands National Lakeshore. The fourth side adjoined Weegwasi's land. It had a stunning view of Eagle Island and Sand Island. While it was not on the water, it was an easy walk to the cliffs above the surf, over acre-sized flat rocks characteristic of Canadian Shield.

It should not have been there. This whole stretch of the Wisconsin peninsula was protected land. But men who hunt cape buffalo and wildebeest, and who play in circuit boards, often make their own rules. It is possible the house sat on a piece of privately owned homestead that had been grandfathered in when the federal government swallowed this whole stretch of rocky coastline, with the sea caves below, groaning in storms, throwing up geysers of white water through blowholes in the sandstone. There were privately owned parcels like that on Sand Island.

It's also possible it had been acquired at some point from the tribe, maybe on a lease agreement. Tribal government was not always as pure as the land, as free of corruption, or as immune from the siren call of money.

Whatever the story, it was quite a place. The room in front, with all the trophies, was three stories tall, surrounded by plates of glass the size of billboards. The middle of the room was a stone fireplace easily big enough to embrace birch logs six feet long.

The deck in front of this room sprawled for a hundred feet in three directions and could have contained three or four hundred people for cocktails.

But there were no cocktails and no parties. There was a virus instead, and everyone had gone into hiding. This place on the lake was so vacant it was ghostly.

If the residents didn't get back soon, they wouldn't get back at all. There was only one road coming through the reservation, and in two places it ran through a marsh. For probably two years or more the marsh had been rising, and so had the road, built up with countless truckloads of gravel. But the marsh was winning, and the road could go no higher unless it became a bridge or a levee.

Just driving in, even before he got to the house, Radisson could see a motive. An enormous investment in glass and stone and steel was about to become the victim of a warming climate—unless Charlie Weegwasi would agree to a new route in.

The mailbox was crammed with offers and ads, but no bills. Radisson looked at the dates and realized the house had been unoccupied since before Charlie Weegwasi had disappeared. That made it unlikely Douglas Kincaid had been dancing around Charlie's house in a chicken suit, but people like Kincaid didn't do anything themselves. They hired it done.

When he dialed Kincaid's number, he could hear the phone ringing inside the big lodge. What he needed was a cell phone number, and he didn't have one. Jackie Beeksma could find out pretty much anything, and lock it into her fine mind until the day she died. But this time she had been stymied.

"Any luck?" he asked when he called the office. "This place is deserted."

"Douglas Kincaid also serves on the board of Fairmont MicroSystems," Jackie said. "They must have some way of contacting him, but they aren't saying. The executive assistant to the CEO said Kincaid was in the Caribbean somewhere, on an island. She had an address but not a number. She said his normal cell phone doesn't work there."

"Hiding out from the virus," Radisson said. "He shoots buffalo but runs from bugs. Guess he doesn't like a fair fight."

"I could overnight a letter to him. Ask him to call. I don't know if it would get to him."

"I have a better idea," Radisson said. And he hung up. From his truck he took a clipboard and sheet of paper and a marking pen. He printed in large letters: "Mr. Kincaid. Please call Bayfield County Sheriff's Office. Important."

The house, the deck, the garage, and even the mailbox were festooned with cameras. Radisson walked around to each, holding up his sign. The cameras were either monitored by Kincaid or by some security company who could reach him. Probably. It was worth a try.

On his way back he called James Deperry, the contractor husband of the social worker in Red Cliff.

"Don't worry, Sheriff. I'm not going to build that thing," Deperry said.

"You mean the road."

"Sure. I know the rules."

"I don't think Charlie Weegwasi would want a road, if he's still alive."

"Well, he gave Douglass Kincaid an easement. But that's not the problem."

"Are you sure? I can't see Charlie doing that."

"Mr. Kincaid told me himself," Deperry explained. "He said his lawyer had already recorded the easement and everything was on the up and up. He just needed someone who could build the road."

"Huh."

"I was skeptical too, so I called the county clerk and the easement is there. But that's not the problem."

"What's the problem?"

"The whole back half of Charlie's land, maybe sixty acres, is marsh on one side and shield on the other. The marsh side is what touches Kincaid's land. It could be filled in but it's wetland, and I'm pretty sure you have to get permission from the DNR to mess with that. He wants me to just charge ahead and not tell anyone. He said he'd pay any fines. But I've been thinking about it, and it's not worth the risk."

"Do you know how I can get in touch with Mr. Kincaid?"

"He said he was going away and wouldn't be back until next month. That's all I know."

"Do you know when that easement was signed? Was it before or after Charlie disappeared?"

"Oh, it was before, but not much, I think. A day or two maybe."

"I don't think you should build that road until I can find out what's going on. Some of this doesn't make any sense."

Radisson had just hung up when the call came through from Grant, still standing with his back to the big tree, all around him the signs of a struggle with wolves, and blood on the ground.

"Sam," Radisson shouted. "I just ran into the darndest thing."

"Well, you know what, Lewis? Me too."

"There's a big house just north of Weegwasi's land. I didn't even know it was here. It's like a mansion. Charlie could have made it this far, but nobody has been home here since before he disappeared. I checked all the doors and windows and there's no sign of forced entry. There are security cameras and alarms everywhere."

"Are you still there?"

"Yeah. Just getting ready to go."

"Would you stop by Weegwasi's place? There's something here you need to see."

FIFTEEN

B Y THE time Radisson had followed Grant's snowshoe tracks to the double tree, only one wolf was left, sitting behind a bush, looking more or less disinterested.

"I don't think they're hungry," Grant said. "Good thing, too."

"Just in case, I brought this." The sheriff un-slung the big sniper rifle from his shoulder and leaned it against the tree.

"It's illegal to shoot a wolf. And unwise. We are all brothers and sisters."

"Well, I came prepared for a family squabble," Radisson quipped. "And speaking of squabbles, it looks like there was one right here."

Granted pointed to several drops of blood. "I didn't want to mess around until you got here."

Radisson took off his snowshoes, got down on his knees, and opened his evidence case. It contained rubber gloves and bags and bottles and vials of stuff. There was a camera too, but the sheriff had filmed the scene on his cell phone as soon as he arrived. Near the tree, the snow had been worn away by the struggle, leaving a two-square-foot area of pine needles and dry, brown leaves.

There were spots of blood and Radisson slid a couple of stained leaves into a bottle.

The snow around the bare spot was pink with blood that had been stirred in, but when Radisson lifted an unstained loaf of snow, underneath he discovered a large pool of dark, frozen blood. He whistled.

"Sam, the snow has covered a bunch of it, but there is a lot of blood here. A lot." He began picking up pieces of blood with tweezers and putting them into bags and bottles.

"I couldn't find a body."

'Well, there would be about a foot of snow on it." Radisson looked around. He walked over to a couple of high spots and kicked through them. "Would wolves drag a carcass away?"

"Probably. They might fight over it and tear pieces off and carry them away. Coyotes too. Wolverines. God knows what else."

Finally, Radisson stretched his big body to its full height and looked out toward the horizon. "I'm sorry, Sam. It doesn't look good."

"No, it doesn't."

"Nice way to murder someone, huh? Let the wolves do the wet work."

"That little old man wouldn't have lasted long."

"Looks like he put up a pretty good fight."

"If someone just scared him and this happened, is there any crime? Even if we catch him, he could say it was just a joke."

"Negligent homicide, maybe. Like drunk driving. Big fine and six months to five years. But it would be a hard case to prove. Still, we need to finish the investigation. The rich guy up on the lake recorded an easement just before Charlie disappeared."

"Charlie couldn't read an easement and couldn't sign one. Besides, he'd never knowingly do that."

"That's what I figured. Douglas Kincaid has some explaining to do." Radisson scanned the horizon and sighed deeply. "I need to visit Weegwasi's grandson tomorrow to tell him what we found. Want to come?"

"Sure."

"We still need to follow up on any big collectors of his baskets. They have a lot to gain from all this bloody snow. I sure hope we can find who—or what—made those tracks."

"I'm tired, Lewis. It's getting late. Let's go home."

"To your recliner in a smoky cabin?"

"I've had worse."

"I need to stop at Weegwasi's place and collect whatever I can find that will have his DNA. It won't take long. I would appreciate it if you would stay until I'm done. His place gives me the creeps."

SIXTEEN

Sam Grant was standing in the parking lot of the Red Cliff Community Health Center, thermos in hand, when Jacob Dewberry drove up in a particularly old police cruiser.

"I see you get the best car," Grant said. "I'm Sam Grant. Thanks for meeting me. I brought coffee."

"I'm bottom of the totem pole," Jacob explained.

"That's what I understand. Gokee is impressed with you, though."

"Good to hear. Sorry to meet you outside. The restaurants are closed."

"Quite a year, huh?"

Grant introduced himself as being from the Bear Clan, but raised both on and off the reservation. He mentioned his grandmother, his mentor, who died some years ago.

"I know about you," Dewberry said. "Everyone does. It's not hard to get information. You are the son of Standing Bear, head of the Bear Clan."

"I can't say that without disparaging my late mother, who was married to another man."

"I understand. But Standing Bear claims you as his son."

"He claims a lot of sons on the reservation, and probably he's mostly right."

"I am told he was a big, influential man, like yourself."

"He's a lot bigger than me," Grant laughed. "He's huge, actually."

"Yeah. Women like big men," Dewberry said. He said it with just a whisper of sadness, but Grant picked up on it.

"Well, not just big men," he said.

Dewberry told Grant he was from the Crane Clan, born to the Loon Clan. He talked about his family and growing up at Lac Court Oreilles. The whole conversation would seem inefficient to a white person, which it was, but an Ojibwe didn't like to talk business without a proper introduction of clans and families.

Sam Grant had been a reporter most of his life, and it did not take him long to size up new acquaintances. Maybe it was just intuition. Maybe it was something more. In any case, he almost instantly liked this this new young patrolman.

"I was hoping you could tell me something about that plane crash," Grant said. "The sheriff is keen to know and the feds don't share any information."

"I've been out there, but I have to stay away from the plane."

"Is it just a drug thing?"

"I don't think they found any drugs or money. I think they are stumped."

"Huh."

"They may not be telling the sheriff anything because they don't know anything."

"And what about you?"

"I don't know anything either. Nobody tells me anything."

While he was talking, Dewberry kept glancing over Grant's shoulder. "Are you waiting for someone?" Sam asked.

Jacob blushed. "No. Not really. There's a woman who works in there. I thought I might see her come out for lunch."

"Ahhhh, I see. That's why you wanted to meet here. What's her name?"

"Janice. That's all I know. She's new. An intern."

"Good looking?"

Jacob blushed again. "Yeah.

"Interns sometimes don't stay around long. Better move fast." Dewberry looked down, shuffled his feet and didn't say anything. "I'll tell you what, Jacob. What if I got you Janice's name and number, and a little information? You might owe me, right? You know, return the favor."

"Sure, if it's not illegal. Are you calling right now?"

"Have to," Grant said, dialing a number. "My memory is shot. I won't remember to do it later. I used to know a woman who worked there. Bette Smallwood. Through her I met some others."

"How can you remember them? Or the number?"

"It's complicated," Grant said. "I remember old stuff, not new stuff."

Grant made a connection and after some small talk asked the voice on the other end if she knew an intern named Janice. "There is a new patrolman on the force who has seen her and thinks she's cute, but he doesn't have her last name or number.... Uh-huh ... Yeah, he's cute too.... I would think so.... Is she, you know, unattached?... Yeah, that's good.... Uh-huh ... Good family? ... Yeah? Oh, he is I'd say twenty-two or twenty-three. Nice-looking. Clean-cut. A little shy, maybe. Loon and Crane. From Lac Court Oreilles. A veteran. Good family ... Uh-huh ... Wait, I'm writing this down.... I'll tell him. You tell Janice I called and that Jacob Dewberry thinks she's cute. That should get her thinking.... Okay, will do. And thanks so much"

Grant tore off a piece of paper and handed it to Dewberry. "Janice Newman. Part Cree but not enrolled. That's her number. She's a senior at Wisconsin Eau Claire. A nursing student. Here for six months."

"Unbelievable," Dewberry said. "They told me you were once a hot-shot reporter, but that was amazing. I could learn a lot from you."

"Let me show you what is amazing." Grant stepped up and stood very close to Dewberry, his head down. "You are carrying something. A very heavy weight. You know something that you have told nobody else, so you carry the weight alone."

Dewberry took a deep breath. "You are reading my spirit. I have heard about this."

"You are easy to read, my young friend. I could feel your troubled spirit the moment you drove up, before you ever left your car. But you are good man ... with a secret."

"Can you tell what it is?"

"It is a conflict inside you. I don't know what. I know you have never had a conflict like this before."

"No."

"Tell me." Grant switched to his low, soft voice

"I can't."

"Do not carry this load alone. Tell only me. Carry just half the load."

"I would love to, but I can't."

"You can trust me."

"I'm sorry."

"The weight of the load you carry is pushing you down, into the ground. Can you feel it?"

"Stop whatever you are doing."

"It's okay. It is warm in the ground. It is very relaxing."

"You are trying to hypnotize me."

"I am trying to share your load."

"I can't."

"It's about the airplane."

"How can you know that?"

"There is something in your pocket. Your pants pocket. The left pocket."

"For God's sake," Dewberry yelled and broke away. He cursed and walked in little circles by his car. "Leave me alone. You are some kind of witch."

"I am your friend, Jacob. I know your spirit and I like it. You will come to see that I am your friend. You already feel it. You know that what I am saying is true."

"You were trying to hypnotize me so I would tell you things I don't want to."

"No, I wasn't. I don't do things like that anymore because, evidently, I get punished. I can't take any more punishment or I will be blind, deaf and lame."

"I can see that."

"Jacob, I was trying to heal you. That's all."

"I'm not sick."

"Then you believe that you are in harmony? That your spirit is untroubled and open to the beauty of life?"

"Well, no."

"Before you meet Janice Newman, you should find harmony."

"How do I do that?"

"Come stand here and close your eyes. Listen to me. Listen to my voice as I speak and imagine that I am drawing away, and my voice is becoming distant. You are being left alone, but you feel safe. You know you are safe here. You are beginning to sink back down into the earth. A well is opening around you and the bottom is going down until you are nearly underground. Warm, sweet-smelling water is coming in around you, filling the well. It is like being in a warm bath. It is very comfortable and very safe. Imagine the heavy thing in your heart. Remove it and hold it in one of your hands. Open your other hand and see that there is a box in it. Put the heavy thing in the box and put it down. It will stay in the well while you begin to rise. The water is running off. The well is filling with earth under your feet. The box is buried and you are rising to the top again. Now you are here, right back where you were. Open your eyes, Jacob."

"That's it?" the young man asked.

"That's it. How do you feel?"

"Great," Dewberry said. Then he thought about it for a minute. "Really great, actually. Wow. Can you teach me to do that?"

"Would you like to learn?"

"Yeah. I might."

"When I was a boy, I watched my grandmother do this many times. I suppose some would call it hypnosis. I think it's more like getting someone to focus on the thing that is bothering him. I think when he does that, he can see that the thing is manageable."

"So you weren't trying to pump me for information?"

"I think it would be better if you shared your burden, but I won't press it."

"I need time to think."

"Sure. I will call you tomorrow."

"Thanks for … for whatever you did."

"Call her."

"I will."

Grant turned to leave when Dewberry called out to him. "Mr. Grant, wait a minute." He took the lump from his pocket. "Take this. I can't carry it anymore. Call me tomorrow."

Grant held the lump in his hand until Dewberry was gone, and then opened it slowly. The lump was a little piece of shiny metal. He turned it over and over. It was a broken thumb-throttle lever from a snowmobile.

SEVENTEEN

"**M**R. PATKI, this is Sam Grant calling. Some years ago, I visited you and wrote an article for the Chicago Tribune Sunday magazine. Do you remember that?"

"Mr. Grant, it's framed and hanging on my wall. What can I do for you?"

"As I recall, you dealt in a lot of pueblo pottery but also in native baskets. Have you ever heard of Charlie Weegwasi?"

"Of course. Ojibwe basket maker. Are you buying or selling?"

"Which would you prefer?"

"I'll buy anything you have, if it's legit. Can't sell you anything."

"Why is that, Mr. Patki?"

"Collectors snap them up. Weegwasi is getting old, so everyone knows the supply is limited. It's like those Frog Woman pots. The original ones. Nampeyo. Remember what a craze they were? She was a wonderful Hopi potter, God rest her soul. But as she got older, the price of her pots got all out of hand. Lots of collectors made a ton of money, for a while. If the pot had a frog drawn on the bottom, it was worth more than gold.

"Then Frog Woman pots flooded the market, all of them with the frog on the bottom. Sisters, daughters, granddaughters, grandsons, sons-in-law, grandsons-in-law. Hell, a lot of Frog Woman pots out there weren't even made by a woman."

"You think that will happen with Weegwasi?"

"Nobody can duplicate his baskets. So as he gets older, the prices just go up and up. There is one woman in Texas who buys everything I get, sight unseen. She probably has the same agreement with other dealers, too."

"That's why I was calling, actually. Do you think you can put me in touch with her? I'd like to talk with a big Weegwasi collector."

"You still writing? What's your interest in Weegwasi?"

"I'm Ojibwe."

"I'm Hopi. So what? I prefer Acoma pottery."

"If I told you why I'm interested … if I told you something really important about Charlie Weegwasi, would you tell me your buyer?"

"Depends. But I'm intrigued."

"Weegwasi is missing. It doesn't look good."

"You're kidding me."

"I'm helping the sheriff with the investigation because he needs someone with Ojibwe contacts."

"My God."

"It's true."

"Weegwasi dead?"

"Well just missing, right now."

"My God. I don't even know how to feel about that. The value of his baskets will go way up. That's good for me. But I won't get any more baskets. That's bad for me. My God."

"I would appreciate it if you wouldn't spread that around. It's an open investigation."

"Why would I tell anyone? Do you realize what an advantage this gives me?"

"I was hoping you would be grateful."

"I am, Mr. Grant. I'll tell you anything you want to know. I don't even care about my agreement with Mrs. King. I am now keeping every basket I can get."

"You're not afraid of a market flooded with imitations?"

"No, no. That's why collectors really like Weegwasi. He has some way of infusing his wood with a copper color. Nobody knows how he does it. And nobody has ever duplicated it. Every pueblo has special sources of clay that fire up with unique colors. But every potter in the pueblo knows how to find the clay and how to handle it. It's not like that with Weegwasi."

"And he is still using pine root for lashing."

"Well, that's the thing, Mr. Grant. If you want art, true art, there are a lot better artists than most of these traditional potters and basket makers. I think the Navajo guy, Bob Lansing, makes unbelievable pots, but they sell for a fraction of their value. Collectors don't want modern stuff. They want things made in the traditional way, using traditional materials and motifs. They know the traditional skills are dying. In most tribes, we're seeing the last generation of artisans. It's all about supply and demand. Charlie never made more than about fifty baskets a year. And now nobody will be making any. I don't know how to feel about that."

"This Mrs. King, is she related to the ranch family?"

"Maybe. In some way. A relative or a wife. I can tell you she has the money. She never bats an eye at anything I ask."

"Has she been buying a lot more lately?"

"A lot more, yeah. Everything I can find."

"I wonder why?"

"She's a shrewd old woman. Charlie is eighty, at least. She sees the handwriting on the wall."

"Does she ever sell, or does she just buy?"

"I have never known her to sell anything. Maybe to a museum, something special. She's a hoarder when it comes to native crafts. My God, her basket collection is going to be worth millions."

EIGHTEEN

MRS. KING didn't sound like the sort of woman inclined to waste time on the phone with an old reporter who had one eye completely closed now, and a mouth that didn't want to move. He had better say something interesting, and say it fast, or Mrs. King would cut him short. It wouldn't be the way an Easterner does it, with perfect diction, and the sort of supercilious voice that suspects you are poor, uneducated and probably Republican. No, it would be that kind of melodious Texas putdown, drawled out in a syrupy voice that ends by saying "thank you for calling" in such a way that it is clear you are just a heap of white trash.

So Grant quickly introduced himself and said, "Mrs. King, I am working for the sheriff of Bayfield County, Wisconsin, on a case involving a Mr. Charlie Weegwasi. I understand you know him."

"Weegwasi? The basket maker?"

"Yes, ma'am."

"I don't know him really, but I collect his baskets."

"Have you ever met him?"

"Two or three times, at that powwow they have on the reservation by the lake. It's my son Mathew who really knows him. What's this about?"

"Mr. Weegwasi is missing and we are trying to find his friends and acquaintances, agents and buyers, who he might have contacted."

"Well, he wouldn't call me. Why would he?"

"I don't know, Mrs. King. Maybe to sell some baskets. You know, raise some money." Grant was winging it now, just trying to keep her on the phone until something useful might come out.

"He would call Mathew, if he called anyone at all. I doubt he has a phone."

"So he knows your son?"

"Mathew is the basket collector. I think anyone would say he is an expert. I prefer pottery."

"I see. How can I get in touch with Mathew?"

"He's in Wisconsin now. In Madison. He's attending a conference on post-contact changes in Ojibwe culture. He does a lot of that sort of thing."

"How long has he been in Wisconsin?"

"I don't know. Maybe a week. He is a 45-year-old man, Mr. Grant. I don't tuck him in. I don't see where this is going."

"So the baskets you buy from Mr. Patki, for example, are really Mathew's baskets?"

"Of course not. They are OUR baskets."

"You have been buying a lot more lately, I understand."

"Mr. Grant, I am not a fool. I make careful investments after a great deal of examination. Charlie Weegwasi is getting old. His production is diminishing. He is a good value, so Mathew and I have focused on him."

"Would you by any chance ... "

"Mr. Grant. You are wasting my time. You and I both know you have called because the value of my collection will go up if something happens to Mr. Weegwasi. That makes me a suspect because I have a motive."

"Yes, ma'am. That's about the size of it."

"Mr. Grant, the value of my baskets is irrelevant. I don't sell. Ever. But what if did? So what? The increase in value might be enough to pay for one of my summer barbecues. Do you understand what I am saying, Mr. Grant?"

"Oh yes, ma'am."

"Good. If you have anything else, you can contact Mathew, or I can refer you to my lawyer at Baker Botts. Goodbye Mr. Grant. Thank you for calling."

There it was, and sure enough, Grant felt like a heap of white trash. He shuffled into the bedroom and looked at himself in Mrs. Brebeuf's smoky mirror.

Bell's palsy, the doctor had called it, a temporary paralysis of the face that causes an eye to close, along with disruptions in the muscles around the mouth and cheeks. Probably related to Grant's brain trauma, the doctor said.

It will get better… in a month or a year. Maybe two. Nobody knows what causes it or why it suddenly goes away.

"In the meantime, you should be careful," the doctor warned. "With one eye closed, you don't have any depth perception."

Grant explained that he lived about ten miles deep in the Bad River forest, in a three-room house with a wood stove and an outhouse. "Depth perception," he said, "is one of the many things I do not need."

NINETEEN

SNOW WAS blowing across the road at hurricane velocity, and Grant was happy to drive no farther than the Lake Superior Visitor Center. Radisson was waiting there, his truck idling and wipers going.

"What a storm," Grant huffed, climbing in.

"Just wind now, but snow is coming in tonight. We need to make this a fast trip." Radisson steered back onto Highway 10, his rear wheels sliding as he did.

Grant told Radisson about his conversation with Mr. Patki, to the extent he could remember it. He had taken notes, but he didn't know where they were.

Mrs. King came up next. He rummaged through his pockets for the notes, found them and gave a more thorough report.

"What do you think?" Grant asked. "Her son was in the state. There's motive and opportunity."

"Mathew King. He sounds guilty."

"What?"

"Guilty name."

"That's a little thin, Lewis."

"You can over-think these things. Besides, just 'cause mom doesn't need the money doesn't mean sonny boy isn't up to his neck in gambling debt."

"Well, if you have it solved, I can go home."

"All kidding aside, we've established that collectors know they will benefit from Weegwasi's disappearance, and one of them was here, in the state. It's not much, but you can't rule it out. I think I should have a talk with this Mathew King."

"What's new on the plane crash?"

"Not much. They're taking the plane to Madison for more study, but it looks to have been in good condition and well maintained. So they're ruling out an emergency landing."

"That means it was bringing in dope or picking up money," Grant said. "Why else would you land on four feet of snow in a remote spot on an Indian reservation?"

"There was no dope and no money in the plane. But whoever was waiting for it could have taken it. That would be a motive for whacking the pilot in the head." Grant nodded, but Radisson seemed unsure.

"Let's work it from the beginning," Grant said. "Two guys set off in a small plane from Thunder Bay to Raspberry Bay. They must have somebody waiting for them. That bay is the middle of nowhere. They're either bringing in something or taking out something."

"Or someone," Radisson said. "The passenger was probably Russian. He was dressed in a suit and cashmere overcoat, handmade in Moscow. Very expensive."

"Bigwig in the Russian mafia, trying to sneak in?"

"Maybe. But there was no luggage. And why would you dress like that? And who the hell was he? He was carrying no identification papers of any kind. His prints aren't on file. And his face was messed up too much to run him through the facial recognition system. The pilot was a working stiff in Canada with a nice wife and two kids. He was just making a living. His wife said he made the run about every three months. She didn't even know it was illegal."

"Same passenger every time?"

"She didn't know. Her husband didn't talk about it and she was never there when he took off."

"So the plane could have been loaded with contraband."

"Could have been."

Grant summarized what might have happened. "The plane crashes in the deep snow. The Russian is killed but the pilot survives. The pilot is a nobody to whomever is waiting for that plane, and he knows too much. So he gets his head conked. Whatever was on the plane, dope maybe, is removed. The passenger's papers are removed too, and his luggage and anything that would identify him. Then the person or people who were waiting for the plane to take off. No suspects. A crime scene buried in snow. A mystery man in the passenger seat."

"Nothing to go on," Radisson stated flatly.

"Well," Grant mused, "There might be something, but I don't know yet. There is a new patrolman working for Red Cliff. Jacob Dewberry. Seems like a dedicated young man. A veteran. I think he may have something."

"What?"

"I don't know yet. It's something he's afraid to talk about. I don't know why."

"Another *wiindigoog* running around? I'm telling you, I don't know how you people ever get anything done."

"We get things done … carefully, Lewis. We don't go barging around like a bunch of storm troopers. The reservation is a big family."

"Well, let me know what you find out."

"I will. In the meantime, back to Charlie's disappearance. This James Birch. Are we just notifying him today, or is this an interrogation?"

"I'm pretty sure we know what happened to his granddad. It's preliminary until we get the tests back on those blood samples, but he's the only next-of-kin and needs to be notified. But there are still those tracks in the snow. That part is unresolved. I'm not sure we should tell him about those."

"It's hard to figure why Birch would be involved in anything that would have gotten Charlie killed," Grant said. "He cared for and assisted the old man for years. But there is something that bothers me. If my granddad were missing, I'd be out there every day, combing the woods, hollering, trying to find out what happened. Birch hasn't been there once as far as I can tell. And neither has the Bear Clan, which would have normally organized an impressive search. It's like everyone is scared. Or else they already knew Charlie was a goner."

"Look at this," Radisson said, and then whistled. They were passing Pigeon Lake on County N. "We probably used a hundred loads of gravel to build up this road, and it's still just an inch or two above the water." All the houses and garages along the lakefront were submerged up to their windowsills. Some were even deeper.

"Breaks your heart, doesn't it?" Sam groaned. "People's dreams—their homes or cottages—gone forever."

"The continental divide is just a mile or so south of us. Everything on the other side drains into the Mississippi River system and the Gulf of Mexico. But everything on this side drains into Lake Superior and out through the Great Lakes into the North Atlantic. Somehow, a lot of these interior lakes are connected underground with Lake Superior. As it goes up, they go up."

"So much destruction already. And it's just begun."

"I know a lot of people who have places high up above the lakes. They think they're safe. What they don't understand is that they'll be cut off. All these roads run through the lowest places. We probably have two dozen Bayfield County roads under water right now. Nothing we can do but haul gravel and hope we can keep ahead of it. But it's expensive, and in lots of places we're losing the race."

When they arrived at the James Birch house, they found the drive and sidewalks un-shoveled, so they waded onto the porch through knee-deep snow. "Now remember, Grant, this man is going to be bereaved. We can interview him, but be nice."

"No, sir. This man never tried once to go out and find his grandfather. Never lifted a finger. There's something going on, and I'm going to find out what."

It took a long time for the door to swing open, and when it did, inside was James Birch. He had a cast on his left arm and a huge bandage that ran all up and down his right leg. His right wrist was wrapped as well and he had a black eye. "I'm afraid I'm a little slow, gentlemen. Sorry. I slipped on the ice last week and fell down the steps. Broke my arm and tore my leg up. Pulled tendons and stuff. I'm a mess, actually."

Radisson turned to Grant and smiled. Grant smiled back, trying to look especially innocent. "Open mouth, insert foot," the sheriff whispered.

"I have an injured brain," Grant whispered back. "I am not responsible."

TWENTY

Radisson and Grant sat down in a cluttered parlor and tried to think how to begin. You can't exactly tell someone their grandfather was torn apart by wolves and all that's left is a small pond of frozen blood.

"Mr. Birch," Radisson began, "I want to stress that what we are going to tell you is all preliminary. But I am afraid it doesn't look good. We believe we know what happened to Mr. Weegwasi. We believe he was frightened by somebody or something that came to his house in the evening of the first snowfall. We believe he ran from the house out into the storm and died as a result. We have not been able to recover his body. I hope you understand. There is a lot of snow and scavengers and the like. But we have found a good deal of evidence, and we are having tests performed that should enable us to bring some closure. For now. When the snow melts this spring, we may be able to do something more."

James Birch was silent for a few minutes, and then melted into the kind of grief Sam Grant had not seen since the death of his own daughter and the collapse of Jeannie, his wife, years ago. Birch bawled uncontrollably, his body shaking, his lungs gasping for air. Radisson tried to console him. Grant found his way into the kitchen and brought a glass of water. Birch tried to take a drink but choked and spit and started bawling again.

Finally, Grant got up and wandered the house. It was a scene too familiar, and it brought back memories he thought he had put away. His daughter had been shot down on the streets of Milwaukee while she was coming out of a restaurant. She was hit by a stray bullet from a gang fight a block away.

She was a beautiful young woman, away from home for the first time, a freshman at Marquette. She was fun-loving and smart and good with people. She was excited by college. And in an instant, it was all done. Grant would never forget the phone call. Never forget Jeannie's grief. Never forget how they had pulled apart afterward. Grant hardened himself against the pain, and then submerged himself into work. Jeannie had needed the kind of help he couldn't give her, and they were lost.

Looking at James Birch, Grant saw for the first time the gulf between himself and his wife, even after all these years. A gulf of pain and blame, of unfinished expectations and unrealized dreams. What had he been thinking? He could see the whole sequence now, how one thing had led to another, the inevitability of it all.

He had been waiting for Jeannie to get over it and waiting for himself to get over it, and now he saw that it was the kind of grief you never get over, because his daughter's absence was something that happened anew every day. It didn't go away. She was absent today and she would be absent again tomorrow and the next day.

Grant roamed the front room while Birch cried. He saw the Weegwasi baskets, half a dozen, on a shelf over the fireplace. He picked up the pictures on the piano, one by one. Some were of Birch, an only child, and his parents. Some were Birch and his wife and two daughters, about twelve and fourteen. Some were of Weegwasi in different seasons and locations. In one, he is standing in snow and wearing knee-high moccasins.

"Mr. Birch," Grant said softly, "You look just like your mother. Are your wife and daughters not here?"

"They're in Madison," he said, struggling for control. "With my wife's mother."

"Would you like me to call them for you?"

"No. But thank you. I'll do it."

"Forgive me for saying so, Mr. Birch, but your house looks like they have been away for some time."

Birch wiped his eyes and blew his nose and nodded. "A few months," he said. "It's just been so hard. This epidemic. The kids have been out of school. My wife lost her job. I think sometimes I just can't go on."

"And you own some restaurants?"

"Yes." He nodded again.

"That must be a struggle right now. All the closures. All the rules."

"Impossible," he said. "I'm sick with worry. I had to let go almost my whole staff. I don't know what will become of us. And now this."

"I'm so sorry," Grant said.

"I tried to get him into that nice assisted living home in Hayward. But he wouldn't go. I knew something like this would happen."

"Mr. Birch, do you know anyone who would benefit by your grandfather's death?"

"Just the tribe. They get everything. And I know they need the money."

"Do you know whether one of his basket collectors might have come around? A man from Texas, named King. Maybe for a friendly visit?"

"Pops didn't say anything about that."

"How about a Mr. Kincaid. Have you heard of him."

"He visited Pops. I know that because I met him driving out while I was driving in. I stopped him of course, because that was unusual. He gave me his card and said he had talked to granddad about selling or leasing an easement for a road. I laughed. I told him Pops would never do that."

"What did he say?"

"Nothing, I think. He just smiled."

"Did he seem angry or anything like that."

"No. Not that I noticed. He was kind of stiff, like a businessman. You know."

Radisson told Birch about the tracks and asked if he thought it might have just been a prank of some kind.

"There are no kids within miles of there," Birch said. "But tracks like that is all it would take. Pops was afraid of spirits. He was like, paranoid, and he was getting worse." Birch started crying again. "I tried to get him to go into that home."

"Mr. Birch, there are no baskets in your grandfather's house. Do you know where he kept them?"

"Nobody does. It's a big secret."

"Nobody? For sure."

"I'll tell you this, the baskets he sells this year are baskets he made a year or two ago. He ages them somehow."

"Is that how they pick up that copper color?" Grant asked.

"I don't know how he does that. Nobody does."

"He's never talked to you about it."

"He had an apprentice for a while. A boy from the tribe. But he went into the army a couple of years ago."

"Do you remember his name?"

"Defoe, I think. Maybe it's Delong. Something like that. Good family."

"Do you know if he's around now, or still in the army?

Birch was crying again and wiping his eyes. "I don't, Mr. Grant. I have no contact with the tribe. Just my visits to Pop's place."

"And the social worker."

"Yes."

"She keeps your grandfather's checkbook."

"Yes. She's as honest as they come."

Grant nodded and thought for a moment. He didn't mind long pauses. He thought they were often very useful. "Your father, was he a Weegwasi or a Birch?"

"Ted Birch. He changed his name when he married Mom."

"She's not Ojibwe?"

"Not enrolled, no. They are both gone. It's just me and Pops." He started bawling again. "Just me now. Oh my God. My God. Why wouldn't he go into that home? Or at least go look at it? It was nice."

Grant showed Radisson the one picture of Weegwasi and the sheriff nodded.

"Mr. Birch," Radisson said, "I see your grandfather is wearing moccasins in the snow. Is that something he did often?"

"Always. They're the best thing. He makes them, and I think he was as proud of his moccasins as he was his baskets. He'd give them as gifts at Christmas."

The grandson broke down again and began shaking violently.

"Mr. Birch, do you mind if I put my hands on your head?"

"You mean, like, pray with me?"

"Sort of like that. It's something my grandmother taught me." Grant pulled a chair up close and put a hand on each side of Birch's head. It was hot and clammy and quivering.

"Mr. Birch, I want you to think of the best time you and your grandfather ever had together. Think back. Take your time. There is no hurry."

"Yes. Okay."

"Picture it in your mind. See it just like you are there right now. Can you do that?"

"Yes."

"Are you at his cabin?"

"Yes."

"What are you doing?"

"We're stripping bark from a tree, with a club. He's telling me stories about my dad, when he was a child, living there at Pop's house. Funny stories. We're both laughing so hard."

"Can you picture his face, with that smile on it, that laugh?"

"Yes."

"Hold that face in your mind. Now imagine that he gets up and touches your head. Just touches it, like this, and starts walking away. Walking to the west. Can you do that?"

"Yes."

"He waves goodbye to you now. He still has that smile on his face. He is happy. Happy! He is beyond pain, beyond care. Can you wave goodbye to him?"

"I'm not sure." Birch broke down again and Grant released his head.

"You keep trying. Keep picturing him. Keep remembering him on that happy day. Until you can wave goodbye."

All the way home Radisson talked about the depth of grief like he had never seen before. Talked about the tragedy. Sometimes the sheriff was angry. Sometimes he was sad.

Grant said nothing.

TWENTY-ONE

JACOB DEWBERRY didn't usually answer calls to his cell phone when he didn't recognize the caller. For some reason, he thought he should this time.

"This is Janice Newman." The voice on the phone didn't sound cheery.

Dewberry grimaced. While he really wanted to talk to her, he hated it that she was making the first call instead of him, hated it because it made him look weak, and hated it because no woman ever made such a call without punishing you for it later.

"Oh, yeah. Hi," he said.

"Were you ever going to call me?"

"Sure," he said.

"You don't tell someone to tell someone you think they're cute and then not call. It's rude."

"I'm sorry," he said. "I wanted to. I've been pretty busy … working on a big case. That is, we're working on a big case. The police department."

"That plane crash?"

"Yes, ma'am. How'd you get my number?"

"I called the department. They said you were out but gave me your cell number."

"I'm out at the crash site. I'm an evidence technician."

"What's that mean, exactly?"

"Ma'am, I'll tell you the truth. I'm not sure."

"Don't call me ma'am. It makes me sound old. I'm twenty-two."

"Yes, ma'am. I mean … "

"How old are you?"

"Twenty-three," he said.

"You sure? I don't date old guys."

"Yes, ma'am. I mean no, ma'am. I mean … I'm twenty-three."

"You married?"

"Oh, no … "

"Ever been married? Got any kids?"

"I've hardly dated. I was in the army. Four years. Overseas. I just got back a year ago."

"I hear you're a little shy."

"No, ma'am. Not really."

"That's what they say."

"They are not always correct, ma'am."

"Ma'am, ma'am, ma'am. I don't know, Jacob Dewberry. You make me call you and then you talk to me like I'm an old woman. It's a good thing you have a nice name."

"Thank you. I wish I had a different name. It's a lot to live up to."

"You're not a sweet Dewberry?"

"It's a little embarrassing. I'm someone who would rather under-promise and then over-deliver."

She laughed. "That's pretty good."

"I saw you when you people from the clinic gave a COVID presentation to the police department."

"I saw you, too. You were eyeing me up. I know who you are. About five-ten, short dark hair, dark eyes, nice smile. A really, really nice complexion. Like satin. I'm jealous."

"Yes, ma'am. I mean, that sounds like me."

"So?"

"Is it my turn?"

"Yes. And it better be good. You made me call first."

"Okay. Let's see. You are five-two or five-three. Short, reddish hair. Blue eyes that kind of sparkle when you smile, which is a lot. You seem happy, and I like that. You have this way you walk. It's kind of girlish but kind of sassy. Lots of confidence. I like that, too. You have a tattoo on your left arm, but most of it was hidden under the short sleeves of your scrubs. I'd say it's probably a tiger kitten. You look intelligent. You look a little impatient. I think you were a bit put out by that woman on your right. You have a really nice figure. Your legs are thin but athletic. You have the calf muscles of someone who rides a bicycle. A lot. You were in blue scrubs with pink shoes that have white laces. You had on very little makeup and no lipstick. But you don't need makeup. You have great skin and fashion model eyebrows and a really, really hot mouth."

There was a very, very long silence, and Dewberry was wishing he'd left off that last part.

"Wow," she said. "That was something."

"I could go on. I'm pretty observant."

"I guess."

"I have a good memory, too. But I cheat. I have to confess. I filmed you with my body cam."

"You filmed me?" She laughed. "Is that even legal?"

"I thought you were cute, so I kicked on my camera."

"And how many women have you filmed with your body camera?"

"Counting you, one. I just got it last month. I was a part-timer before that, and part-timers don't get cameras."

"How many times have you watched it?"

"A few. It's kind of what I do, in the evening. I have dash cams in my cruiser and my pickup. When I'm out of my vehicles, I often use my phone. I film everything, all day. Then in the evening I play the films to see what I might have missed. It's kind of like training, to help me be more observant."

"You take your police work pretty seriously."

"Yes ma'am, I do. But that's not really it. I just think the world moves too fast. It blurs when it goes by. I like to slow it down and look at its parts."

"Really?"

"It takes me a long time to read a book, because I like to spend time with the words."

"Do you read a lot?"

"Yes, ma'am. History, mostly."

"I'm an intern here, you know. Nursing student. I'll only be around a few months. How long is this big case of yours going to last?"

"I was just making excuses for myself, because I hadn't felt ready to call you. The truth is I hardly have anything to do. I spend most of my day just trying to think what else I can do."

"Wow. I like your honesty."

"This man named Sam Grant kind of roped me into this. I usually don't move very fast. You know, with women."

"I've heard lots of stories about him. How long have you known him?"

"What do you hear?"

"Different stuff. Some people say he's been all over the world and is rich. Others say he is a witch."

Dewberry laughed this time. "I'd say witch is pretty close. He's a shaman. But he has a way about him. He seems like someone you can trust."

"So, are we going to meet? How about lunch? Tomorrow. You can pick me up at noon in front of the clinic. I'll just be in scrubs. You can come in your cop clothes. I don't care. I don't cook but I'll bring a salad for the two of us. You bring something to drink. No alcohol. I'll have exactly one hour. Don't try anything funny. Everybody in the clinic will know who I'm with."

"Yes, ma'am. I mean wow. You do move things along."

"I know about shy guys. If I don't move it along, nothing will ever happen."

"That all sounds fine. I look forward to meeting you, Janice."

"You can tell me all about your big case."

"Not much to tell. Maybe I'll just stare into those big blue eyes."

"You can do that, too. If it goes well, I'll expect a kiss. I like kissing."

"Oh, me too," he said. "I mean … what I was trying to say is, I won't try anything. You know. Unless it's okay."

"The point I was making is that with this pandemic, we should be in masks and socially distanced. But I think we have to have a certain level of trust, and a kiss would be okay."

"Yes, ma'am."

"You're calling me ma'am again."

"I'm sorry, Miss Newman. It's the way I was raised. I'm not likely to stop."

TWENTY-TWO

THERE WERE STILL three hours to kill before his dream lunch with his dream date, and it was going to seem like an eternity. Jacob Dewberry, unlike Janice, loved to cook, and had gotten up early to make schnitzel with dill sauce. All that pounding on the boneless pork chops had helped vent some anxiety. What he liked about cooking was the creativity, the opportunity to turn food into art.

He set up three bowls, one with his specially seasoned flour, one with beaten eggs, and one with breadcrumbs. Each cutlet was dipped into each bowl and then fried in hot olive oil. The trick to good schnitzel was getting the temperature right and cooking quickly, just three or four minutes a side, just until the juices run clear.

The dill sauce was made in the same pan when the pork was done. He mixed a little chicken stock into the drippings and then added a cream blend he had made the night before and refrigerated. It was sour cream, Greek yogurt, minced cucumber and dill, with sea salt and just a touch of nutmeg and fresh parsley. He would take the pork in a warm pan with the sauce on the side, a lemon to squeeze on top, and some flatbread. He'd pass it off as just a sandwich to go along with her salad. He would act like it was nothing. He didn't know if she would buy it.

But when he was done cooking, it was still just mid-morning. He drove the cruiser to a good spot on the highway to see if he could catch a *wabiska* speeder. But his patience ran out in about ten minutes.

He drove out past the road that turned into the campground at Raspberry Bay. There were no new tracks in the snow so he drove on. In a few minutes he came to the place where the high water was about to take out the road. He stopped and got out and decided he'd better report it.

"We got maybe an inch to spare," he told Lois, the chief's clerk. "I'm afraid if the water comes across, it's going to wash out a lot of new, expensive gravel."

"I'll get someone on it," she said.

When he got back to the Raspberry Bay turnoff, there were new tracks in the snow. Maybe the feds were back, he thought. If it was just some rubbernecker, checking out the scene of the crime, he'd have to run him off.

The road had been plowed to accommodate all the investigators, but it was still dicey. When he was far enough in to get his first look at the frozen bay, he stopped the cruiser and got out. He didn't have four-wheel drive, so he dared go no farther.

He put on snowshoes and began walking toward the shore. There was someone out there, all right, walking in a circle around where the plane had been. He was carrying something, and when Jacob got close enough, he could see it was a metal detector.

It had to be some amateur treasure hunter, because the FAA had already been all over the bay with metal detectors. He'd explain that to the man, get his identification and send him on his way. It wasn't a big deal. It was still a crime scene, but the plane and everything important had been removed.

Dewberry pulled up his COVID mask and waved to the man, trying to look friendly, which is hard to do when you have a gun on your hip and are dressed like a bandit.

"How you doing?" he said.

The man wore brand-new snowshoes, dark wool pants and a heavy wool coat. He had a black stocking cap and a mask that covered everything but his eyes. He said nothing and continued his search as if Dewberry wasn't even there.

It was possible that his mask and cap covered his ears so much he couldn't hear. Or maybe he had earbuds hooked to the detector. Dewberry stepped closer and touched the man on his back.

"I'm sorry," he said. "This is a crime scene. There were signs on the tree."

"I saw none," the man said. He seemed to have an accent of some kind.

"I don't know where you parked or how you came in. Maybe you missed the signs. Anyway, this is a crime scene and you can't be here. Besides, the feds have been over every inch of this with contraptions just like yours."

The man stood up straight and looked at Dewberry. He looked up and down and then came to rest on Dewberry's eyes. His stare was cold and dismissive.

"Did they find anything?" the man asked. His voice was deep. His accent was ... Jacob thought for a minute. Probably it was Russian.

That thought arrived in Dewberry's head at the exact same moment the barrel of a big revolver arrived at his temple.

"Easy," Jacob said. "Let's keep this friendly."

"Did they find anything?" the deep voice asked again.

Jacob turned his face slightly away from the man and stared into the horizon. "Not much. A few parts maybe. The plane was largely intact."

"Who was in it?"

"The pilot was Canadian. The other man is unidentified."

"Are you certain?" The man pressed the barrel harder against Jacob's head.

"He had no papers of any kind. His prints are not on file."

"There were papers in the plane."

"No, sir. Not even a driver license."

Jacob was thinking he was never going to make his lunch date with Janice Newman. What would she think? How long would it take someone to find his body? They would find his car, but if he fell in the snow, his body could be there until spring.

Jacob risked a quick glance back at the man's heavy brows and dark eyes. He wanted to assess his chances of living through this. The eyes were calm and untroubled. They were the eyes of a man who could kill easily, and without thinking much about it.

The pistol pressed against his head was a Ruger Super Blackhawk. It was built as a .44 magnum but would chamber a .45 Smith & Wesson. It suddenly occurred to Jacob that the .45 round was the Russian competition match round. It was a single-action pistol and needed to be cocked before it was fired.

At that moment, the man cocked it.

"I can't identify you," Jacob said. "I can't see anything but your eyes. You're wearing gloves. There are no prints."

"You could trace my vehicle."

"I haven't even seen your vehicle. I don't know where you parked. I don't know anything about it."

The man paused. "Are you some kind of cop?"

"A tribal patrolman."

"A what?"

"You are on an Indian reservation."

"Indian reservation." The man spat. "Drop your gun belt." Jacob did, instantly. It was a good sign that he might, he just might, live to see Janice Newman's blue eyes. "Do you have a backup?"

"No."

"Pull up your pantlegs. I want to see."

Jacob did that, too.

For the first time the man lowered the gun from Dewberry's head. He pointed toward the open lake, away from shore. "You walk that direction, out into the lake. Walk until I'm this big." The man's fingers showed a space of about two inches. "I'm going to do one more pass around here and leave. If you keep walking and don't turn around, you will be having dinner tonight with your squaw and babies. Otherwise ... "

"Would you please leave my gun here? I'd have to buy a replacement, and I can't afford it."

The man laughed. "Walk."

Jacob took a deep breath and began walking. The first ten to twenty steps were the most dangerous. It was the distance at which the dark-eyed man would shoot him, to avoid blood spatter on his clothing. But if he were a competition shooter, he could wait up to a hundred steps more and then do it just for fun. Just for practice.

It was 150 steps before Jacob Dewberry took his first breath. At the very first instant of relief, the next thing he felt was humiliation. Total humiliation. How could he let himself be disarmed like that? What kind of cop was he? The very worst thing a cop can do is let himself be separated from his gun.

He couldn't even report the incident. He'd be laughed off the force. And anyway, what could he report? He had no idea who the man was or why he was here. No idea what he looked like or what he was driving. He had been humiliated like a green-ass rookie.

Jacob Dewberry walked on for several minutes, turned and discovered the big Russian was gone. He swore a violent oath, and the sound carried out over the ice, out toward the open lake. And nobody heard it and nobody cared.

TWENTY-THREE

WHEN JANICE Newman climbed into Dewberry's truck, she didn't take off her mask. So he didn't take off his.

"Dating is really tough right now, isn't it?" she said. "How do you get to know someone when you can't go out to eat? Can't go to a party or a movie or dancing? Can't even see their face?"

"I suppose, as a nurse, you see a lot of COVID."

"Not so much. Are you afraid of me? In my scrubs?"

"You got on a good heavy coat."

"Still, I could be crawling with virus." She scooted over next to him and put her hand on his arm. "Look, I think there's one crawling onto you right now."

He laughed. "Blue eyes must see better than mine."

"I like your eyes okay." She stared at them for a minute. "They're soft and brown. And intelligent. They are … they are very calm."

"I don't know how they managed that, with you touching my arm."

"So," she said. "Maybe you are not so shy."

"No, ma'am. Lots of people think that, but it's not true. I am … I am careful. That's all."

"Careful?"

"Mr. Grant sort of jumped the gun to set this up. I like to take more time. Observe. Talk to people. Learn. I have a pretty low speed limit."

"Is this uncomfortable for you?"

He laughed. "Ma'am, let me tell you what's uncomfortable. It's having the barrel of a .44 magnum pressed against your head."

He drove past the casino, into the snowbound campground and right down to the edge of the lake. He set the brake but left the engine running so the heater would work. Then he told her the story of his morning.

He didn't think she would believe him. She would probably think he was just some cowboy trying to impress a girl with his dangerous life. But he would never do that. It was a test, like when Sky Woman sent down the Muskrat. Would she go deep enough to see the truth? If not, it was better that they go no further.

"Do you believe me?" he asked.

"Wow," she said. "This date isn't going at all like I expected."

"Would you like me to take you back?"

"Just the opposite. I wish I had more time. You could have been killed." She pulled off her mask and opened a basket with two salads from a gas station. She had applied a little pink lipstick and he could now see that perfect, cream-colored face. Not perfect exactly. Better than perfect. It had just enough oddities to make it exotic. Unforgettable, even.

"I figured the odds were fifty-fifty." Dewberry removed his mask as well and produced his hot pan of pork and two bottles of spring water. "I was in Afghanistan twice. Kabul, Kandahar, Jalalabad. Lots of little villages, too. The people you worry about are the ones who don't say anything. They just walk up and pull a trigger or pull a pin. This guy, he cocked the gun but then started talking, so I thought I had a chance."

"Wow. What a lunch. Did you make this?"

"This morning. I had some time."

"What was he looking for out there on the lake? Look at it." She pointed out across the channel, out toward Madeline Island. "It's like the Arctic."

"I don't know, ma'am."

"Drugs. That's what."

"Maybe. He was using a metal detector, so he must have believed that whatever he was looking for was either metal or was in a metal case."

"Pills would be in a metal case. Opioids. You could put 10,000 in a case no bigger than a briefcase."

"A briefcase," Dewberry repeated. "A briefcase."

"Sure. Probably Krokodil. Do you know about that?"

"No."

"It's Russian, but it all over the reservations now because it's cheap. It's horrible stuff. Horrible. You should see what it does. It turns your skin green and black and scaly, like a crocodile."

"What is it?"

"It's codeine, which is cheap and unregulated in Russia. They mix it with other chemicals and turn it into something called Desomorphine. It's an artificial heroin. Those sleezeballs."

"You know what's funny? When the guy drove out, he passed my cruiser and put my gun belt inside on the seat. That's something, huh? But he stole my dash cam. He saw it and knew it had recorded him driving by. That's pretty smart."

"You didn't get him on your body cam, like you did me." She smiled in a mischievous way. It was kind of sexy.

"I was wearing a coat over it."

"How about now? Are you filming us?"

"I left the camera at home." He pulled his phone out of his pocket. "But I'm recording us. Sorry. I hope you don't think it's creepy. I'm nervous and won't remember half the things you say or how you say them. I want to remember."

"At least you are honest. But that IS a little creepy. I know what you mean, though. Sometimes I will think back on a conversation and I won't be sure anymore what was said."

"Here's the question. A dozen men had searched that wreck site. Yet he knew that whatever he was looking for had not been found. How did he know that?"

"I don't know. How?"

"He knew it because whatever he was looking for would have identified the passenger. He knew it had not been found because the passenger had not been identified. That's it. Probably he was one of the guys waiting for the plane. He's probably the guy who removed all the passenger's identification."

"Why didn't he just take the case when he took the identification?"

"Probably because someone had already taken it. I think that's what happened, but I'm still working it out."

"This is fun."

"I thought it was just some kind of drug delivery. A couple of guys delivering and maybe a couple of guys receiving. But after this morning, I think there is more to it.”

“Why is it always guys?” Janice interjected. “Why do you always presume it’s a man? Can’t a woman do anything? I guess women are incapable of organizing anything as difficult as a crime, right?”

“I didn’t mean that.”

“Yes you did. That’s how you all think.”

He didn’t reply to that because he was thinking about the man with the big pistol and the wrecked plane and the mysterious case. And suddenly, Jacob Dewberry understood everything.

“Of course,” he said.

“I like watching your brain work. Tell me what you think.”

He looked into her young, inquiring face and smiled. “I can’t tell anyone,” he said. “I probably never will.”

“Why?” She almost screamed the word.

“Because,” he said. “I am … a careful man.”

“You said that.” She smiled. “I think you’re afraid of me.”

“Probably.”

“Because you think you don’t know me well enough.”

“Kind of. It’s an Ojibwe thing, Janice. I keep a pretty small circle. I am careful who I let in it because, well, because it’s just about exactly the way I want it already.”

“You called me Janice.”

“Yeah. I guess I did.”

“Careful. I’ll sneak into your circle.”

“Probably.”

She leaned into him and raised her face to his. "I have five minutes. Are you too careful for a kiss?"

TWENTY-FOUR

LEWIS RADISSON had installed a big whiteboard in his office at the Bayfield County Sheriff's Office. In the middle of the board, he had written the name Charlie Weegwasi and had drawn a box around it. There were several more boxes drawn around other names that circled the one in the middle.

There was a box for James Birch. Another one for Douglas Kincaid. A third for "Somebody Defoe." Others were Agnus Deperry, Neighbor Johansen, pot collector Mathew King, and "Unknown Tribal Enforcer."

Jackie Beeksma came in, sat on the table, and swung her bare legs back and forth like a schoolgirl. "Can I play too?"

"This is sheriff's stuff," Radisson said with mock gruffness. "You're a girl." He looked at her for a minute and smiled. Jackie had beautiful, silky legs that always ended in bowling shoes. She got them cheap at Goodwill in Ashland and they were the only things she would wear on her feet. "That's a pretty short skirt for the office."

"What? It's down to my knees."

"Not when you sit like that."

"Are you jealous? Maybe someone will look at your wife."

"Plenty of people will look at you. They do look at you. All the time. I see them."

"Really? Who, for instance?"

"I ain't getting into this. Did you get a copy of that easement?"

"Well, I'm not interested in anyone else, Mr. Sheriff. I've got just the man I want. And he has a brand-new whiteboard in his office. Look at that."

"It's just like on TV," he beamed. "You put the victim right there in the middle and all the suspects around the outside. Then you start drawing lines between them."

"I don't see any lines."

"I haven't gotten to the lines part yet. They're harder."

"You think James Birch is a suspect? That poor man."

"Everyone on this board is someone who had something to gain by Charlie's disappearance. Birch is there only because he could know where Charlie keeps his baskets. He says he doesn't and I believe him. But he has a few baskets that would be worth some money, and he needs money."

"What's this Unknown Tribal Enforcer?"

"The tribe stands to gain the most. It gets everything, including the land, and it also needs the money."

"That's pretty far-fetched."

"Charlie's rich neighbor, this Kincaid guy, he would love to have that land, I bet. He'd pay handsomely for it. So look here. You draw a line between the tribe and Charlie, because the tribe gets the land. Then you draw a between Kincaid and Charlie, because Kincaid needs Charlie's land. But you also draw a line between the tribe and Kincaid, because they have a mutual interest in Charlie's demise. The tribe gets the land and sells it to Kincaid. Good, quick money. See how it works?"

"You have Agnus Deperry up there. I know her. There's not a chance she was involved in anything."

"She has Charlie's checkbook and has handled his money for years. If she's been skimming, she may need to cover her tracks. She knows Charlie and knows his place better than anyone except Birch."

"There is no way she would have been walking around on snowshoes in three feet of snow. Have you seen how big she is?"

"She has a husband who is a contractor. And able-bodied. Let's look at that easement."

Radisson was reading the document when his phone buzzed. "A Mr. Kincaid for you, Sheriff," the operator's voice said.

"Just who I want to talk to," the sheriff said. Jackie skipped out and Radisson picked up.

"Sheriff, this is Douglass Kincaid. I understand you were at my house holding up a sign. You wanted me to call. Is everything okay? With my house?"

"Except for the road in. You are about to lose it, Mr. Kincaid."

"Damn," he said. "Incompetent Indians."

"But that's not what this is about."

"Oh?"

"You have a neighbor named Charlie Weegwasi."

"I do. I've just met him once. By 'neighbor' you mean that my land adjoins his. I'm probably ten miles away by road."

"I understand. But Charlie has disappeared and you were, I understand, one of the last people who saw him."

"Disappeared? What do you mean by disappeared?"

"Just that. We have a pretty good idea what happened to him. It might be a wolf attack. But we have found no body, so we have to check things out."

"There was a wolf at his place when I was there. Standing right at the edge of the clearing. I wanted to shoot him but the old man said no."

"What was the nature of your business with Mr. Weegwasi?"

"You saw it yourself, Sheriff. I'm about to lose the road to my place, the one that comes in from the reservation. I was enquiring about an easement across his land, so I could bring in a road from the other side."

"What was his reaction?"

"He dismissed it out of hand, but we didn't talk any numbers. I told him I would make it worth his while, and I would have my attorney contact him. I met his grandson on the way out and said the same thing."

"Mr. Kincaid, I am holding an easement that was filed last week. Charlie couldn't write, but he drew a little picture of a basket. That was his signature. It's pretty simple, really. Anyone could draw it."

"Sheriff, what is your point? I'm a busy man. I called because I thought something was wrong with my house."

"It is witnessed by a Mary Smith. Mary Smith. There must be about a billion Mary Smiths, huh?"

"I wouldn't know."

"She gives her address as a law office in Milwaukee."

"That would be the attorney who handles my Wisconsin affairs. Wallace Temkin. I have nothing to do with any of that. Sheriff, I met Charlie once. I introduced myself. I told him what I needed and referred him to my attorney. That's it. I have nothing more to add. You need to talk to my attorney. He handled everything else."

"A lawyer isn't going to tell me anything. And he doesn't have to. It just doesn't seem likely to me that Charlie would have been okay with a road through his land."

"Is that easement legal or not?"

"I guess it is. Just a little suspicious."

"I understand there's a problem with the road anyway, because of some wetland issue and because there is too much snow."

"There's a lot of snow. You probably wouldn't know that, Mr. Kincaid. I understand you're on some island somewhere. What do they call it?"

"I don't like snow."

"Nobody does. Not after a while."

"Did you get that plane crash figured out? It flew right over my house."

"You were home?"

"I was literally heading out the door with my driver. It came right over the porch, flying low."

"When I was there, it didn't look like anyone had been at your house for some time. Of course, a lot of snow had fallen."

"I came back to do a virtual board meeting because I keep all my files there. And I needed to pick up a laptop and some papers. I was there probably five hours."

"I've got nothing on the plane crash. It's an FBI thing. And FAA."

"Sheriff, I have to go. I have guests. I have a tee time in one hour and I have other business to do. Since I've been talking to you, I've missed two calls."

"I'm sorry, Mr. Kincaid. I truly am. It must be a burden being so rich."

After the call, Radisson added the name Wallace Timken to his white board and called Sam Grant. Surprisingly, Grant answered on the first ring. "Sam, I need the name of Charlie Weegwasi's apprentice."

"Herald William Defoe. He enlisted two years ago on his eighteenth birthday. Nobody has seen him around. I went to his parents' home but it was deserted. A lot of tribal folks move in with relatives on other reservations in winter."

"Herald Defoe. Sam, I have a new whiteboard in my office, just like they use in those crime shows."

"Wonderful. Now if you could just find a crime."

"Oh, I got a crime all right. Don't know what it is yet. Could be anything from criminal mischief to negligent homicide."

"Did you put the wolves on your board?"

"Nope. They get a pass. But I've got some other good suspects. I just talked to Douglass Kincaid. Didn't learn much, not even where he is. He was too cagey. But I learned he was at his house about the time Charlie disappeared. I wasn't very nice to him. He'll be thinking about me. The really good suspect is Mathew King. I talked to him, too. What an A-hole."

"Takes after his mom."

"He's been in Madison the whole time. Has a rented SUV. He knows Charlie. Knows he's afraid of spirits. He could have cruised up here anytime with a homemade bird suit. And he has the best motive. In his case, we're talking millions. Nobody else has a motive like that."

"Lewis, you sound like a happy man."

"I am happy. This is fun. I needed something interesting. Between the pandemic and all the snow, this has been a heck of a year."

"Yes, it has."

"I have learned the best thing about being a sheriff. Do you want to know what it is?"

"Yes I do, Lewis."

"In court, everyone is innocent until proven guilty. But in a sheriff's office, everyone is guilty until proven innocent. It's way more fun that way."

"I bet."

"Man, I'd like to stick this Mathew King in the hoosegow. That would be a great day. Douglass Kincaid, too. And maybe this Defoe kid. He's probably the only one who knows where Charlie keeps the baskets."

"Probably."

Radisson whistled. "It would be so easy for him to slip in here, scare the hell out of Charlie and then take all the baskets. I'll get Jackie working on him, see if he's still in the army."

"Anything new on the plane crash?"

"What plane crash? Let the FBI mess it up. I've got my own case."

TWENTY-FIVE

IT HAD been a week since the crash and every day, sometimes twice a day, Jacob Dewberry had driven up to Raspberry Bay. Sometimes he walked the mile to the lake. Sometimes he just looked for car tracks. He saw no more of the dark-eyed man with the Russian accent, but he was always wary.

Today he would make the walk, though he had neglected to bring snowshoes. If he followed in the footsteps he had put down before—though they were nearly covered with drifting snow—he thought he'd be okay.

He stepped out of the car, closed his eyes, and just listened. The longer he stood, the more sounds he could distinguish, amplified off the frozen lake. A distant crow. A dog barking way off somewhere. A wolf or coyote on Oak Island, three miles away, or maybe Otter Island, six miles. A small plane above, at 10,000 feet. A snowblower, probably on Madeline Island, twelve miles away.

For sure there was nobody else at Raspberry Bay. He would hear them walking or speaking. In the great stillness of this fine land, he was sure he would hear their heart beat. Yet he felt an uneasiness, and moved off slowly.

On the twenty-minute slog to the lakeshore, the quiet was broken by the crunch his shoes made when they broke through the top layer of hardened snow. And by the wind that bent the tops of the feathery larch trees. Snow like white dust moved across the surface, determined to fill every little depression.

Lake Superior is the largest lake on earth, 32,000 square miles, bigger than all of South Carolina. And it creates its own wind. Creates its own weather, in fact. The lake-effect snow he was wading through was half gone just a few miles south, but it was still building here, with light flurries continuing almost all day, every day.

He was already out of breath when he reached what he thought was the shoreline. In the deep snow it was hard to tell where land and ice merged. He was sure only when he felt the gentle movement of ice underneath his feet, rising and falling on faint waves, like breathing. He raised his binoculars and scanned the area where the crash had been. There was nothing to see. No movement except the blowing snow. Nothing new. No reason to suspect that anything violent and ugly had ever happened here, not since the beginning of time. Not since Sky Woman fell and created it all.

He was suddenly unsure why he was even here, except that he was trying to be a good tribal policeman, trying to do the hard things he knew the others would not. Maybe someday it would pay off, but probably not today.

He turned to go back and, in an instant, he was gone. It was less than an instant. It was just a little piece of an instant. He took one step and the world collapsed beneath him. He was under water so cold it initially seemed hot. And he was sinking fast.

In the first moment of clarity, he cursed his stupidity. He had always come here in snowshoes, and walked safely anywhere he wanted. But his work shoes concentrated his weight onto a few square inches of ice, underneath which there may have been a spring. The lake freezes hard enough to allow for a plowed ice road across from Bayfield to Madeline Island. But along the shoreline, underwater springs often release enough heat to keep the ice thin. You can see these warm spots in the fall because they freeze last. You can look out and see the little circles of open water and know every place there is a spring. But once winter grinds in, it all freezes and looks the same. And then the snow buries it.

A good swimmer, Dewberry began kicking and using his arms like wings, but weighted down with a gun belt and shoes and heavy winter clothes, he made little headway. As his hooded parka became soaked with many pounds of water, he went deeper despite his best efforts.

Finally, he kicked his shoes off and ripped away the coat. But that took time and he kept sinking until his feet touched bottom in probably fifteen feet of water. The pressure squeezed his sinuses and made his ears throb. With all his strength, he crouched on the bottom and then launched himself upward, kicking and flailing, trying desperately to keep himself from taking a breath, though his lungs screamed for him to do that. He came up fast, but what he found was a rigid ice ceiling, not open water. He had missed the hole and hit his head on ice instead.

Dewberry could no longer control the panic. He reached in every direction, patting the frozen underbelly of ice, trying to find a hole. He punched at it. He pushed against it. But every time he did, he sank a few feet and had to kick his way up again. He looked in every direction but it all looked the same. He could see no hole and suddenly realized, in his last coherent seconds, that currents could have carried him many feet away from the hole. He stopped for a moment to record the current pulling on him, and then swam against the current as hard as he could.

At the exact moment of giving up, his head came up through the hole and a breath of air flooded his lungs.

But immediately the current pulled him down again, away from the hole, and he had to start all over. When he found the hole, he went up with outstretched arms, determined to find some way to hold himself against the current. When he tried to lift himself out of the hole, the ice broke under his hands and sent him down again. Finally he burrowed his hands into the deep snow around the hole and was able to get enough of a grasp to keep his head above water.

Using one hand, he released his gun belt and threw it onto the snow-covered ice. His binoculars followed. If he died in this hole, nobody would know. But in spring they might find his things on the ice after the snow melted, and probably guess what had happened.

He tried twice again to get out, but with the same result. The cold water numbed his mind and soon both his energy and vision slipped away. He thought back on the hypnotic well that Sam Grant had talked him into, with the warm, sweet-smelling water coming in like a hot bath. He tried to recreate the feeling he had then. The peace. The safety. The low, calming voice.

But his energy failed and his head slipped under the water. Just as it did that, he thought he saw something and smelled something. A wolf maybe, approaching the hole. Or maybe a bear. So curiosity drove him back up, with one last kick, for one final gasp of air. It was a young bear, shiny black and shaggy, looking at him curiously. Dewberry tried to speak to it, but he was freezing and far past the ability to form words.

The bear lowered its head to smell the dying policeman and to lap up a bit of water. Dewberry grabbed at its head, but the startled animal shook him off and stood up again. When it did, Dewberry reached and grabbed one of the bear's front legs with his right hand, then grabbed the other with his left. The bear stood quietly above him, making no complaint, its massive feet like small snowshoes, safe on the thin ice.

It was wonderful to have hold of something as solid as the bear, but the joy lasted just a second, and then everything went dark. His breathing stopped. His kicking stopped. And Jacob Dewberry began the journey westward.

TWENTY-SIX

THERE WAS a voice in the darkness, but it just made sounds. There was also a soft purring sound and a loud clatter. Jacob Dewberry found it all confusing, so he just waited. He had plenty of time now. He was warm and comfortable. He relaxed and listened, and soon the voice could be heard saying words he understood.

"Jacob Dewberry, are you there? Officer Dewberry?"

Well, of course I'm here, he thought. Where else would I be but right here? Wherever "here" is. He opened his eyes but could see just a blur with a dark smudge running across it. The voice came back and was suddenly talking about a snowplow knocking down some mailbox.

As he waited, he realized that the purring was the sound of an idling car, and the clattering was his teeth. He took several deep breaths to try to stop his teeth, and focused again on the dark smudge. Eventually it resolved into a shotgun, and as he continued to look he realized it was his shotgun, hanging on the safety screen of his patrol car.

"Officer Dewberry?" the voice said again.

He was lying on his back in the rear seat of his cruiser. The car was running and the heater was going and the air around him was almost hot. But his clothes were soaked and his shoes were gone and his feet were numb.

It was a long time before he even tried to make sense of things. And when he did, he could see there was nothing about this that was sensible. The last he remembered he was clinging to the legs of an enormous dog. And then dying in an icy hole. Now here he was in the back seat of his car, relatively warm and totally wet, with an epic headache. Everything between the hole and the car was a blank.

"Officer Dewberry, please phone the office if your radio is not sending."

He sat up, started to pass out and laid down again.

"Officer Dewberry."

His cell phone buzzed but it was soaking wet and by the time he found it in his vest pocket and tried to say hello, it went dead. "Hello" he said anyway, because he wanted to be sure he could speak. "Hello. Hello."

He tried again to sit up, and managed it for a moment, pushing back against the crashing headache. He could see his gun belt and binoculars on the floorboard next to him. There was nothing outside except gathering darkness.

He collapsed onto his back and tried to calculate how long he had been here. Maybe three hours. Maybe four. They were blank hours, just totally gone. So he tried to reconstruct them from what he knew.

There was no way he could have gotten out of the hole in the ice, so somebody must have pulled him out. But who? And how? Approaching a hole in the ice is exceedingly dangerous, and pulling someone out nearly impossible without a rope. But who would have been out here, at this desolate piece of remote lakeshore, with a handy rope?

And who had carried him to his car? Who had laid him in the backseat and started the motor and turned up the heater? Who had brought his gun belt and binoculars? And why?

No single human being could have carried him a mile through deep snow.

"Office Jacob Dewberry. Please respond."

But maybe it wasn't a human. Maybe it was a spirit. A *wiindigoog*. Something huge and strong and oddly benevolent. A spirit might have been invisible, explaining why Dewberry had seen nobody else.

Or it could have been the bear. *Wiindigoog* were known to be shape shifters. Perhaps it had presented itself to him as a bear.

Tracks, he thought. There would be tracks. They would explain everything.

Dewberry sat up and swung his legs onto the floorboard. His body felt stiff and remote, but he was able to pull the handle and open the door and slide out. His feet had no feeling, not even pain. He braced himself against the car and looked around in the evening gloom. He could clearly see the already half-buried tracks he had made when he walked to the lake. There were no other tracks of any kind. No *wiindigoog*, no bear, nothing.

Dewberry closed his eyes tight against the pain in his head. But that did nothing to relieve his bafflement. He was somehow caught up in a miracle. That's what it was. Whatever had happened, it was a miracle. Dewberry had lived an adventurous life, and gone to war twice. But at no other time had he believed that the intervention of a compassionate spirit was the best explanation for his survival.

He rested his eyes for a moment and then reopened them. His vision cleared, but there were still no tracks.

"Office Dewberry," repeated the voice on the radio, sounding increasingly urgent. "Please contact the office. Immediately."

Jacob managed to get the front door open, but his feet did not respond when he ordered them to move. He fell hard against the door and then slipped. His shoulder hit the ground and his head bounced against the hard bottom rim of the open door.

It was several minutes before he was conscious enough to pull himself onto the front floorboard. He reached up and found the mike and pushed the button. It was several more seconds before he realized he was only talking in his mind. There was no sound coming from his mouth.

"Off … " he struggled to get out a word. "Officer Dew … Officer Dewberry. Straw … Raspberry Bay. Ambulance."

TWENTY-SEVEN

ANYTIME AN Ojibwe *wiindigoog* put in a cameo appearance, Sam Grant was the first to hear. Folks just figured he would be involved somehow, or interested, or maybe at fault. The spirit world was a scary place to normal people, but Sam Grant was some kind of shaman, and his uncle was worse. They were plugged into things people shouldn't mess with.

Jacob Dewberry had been taken by ambulance to the Red Cliff tribal clinic, where he had been fussed over by a round-faced nurse practitioner. She had looked at his feet and clucked her tongue. Then she had clucked over his hands and then his face.

Dewberry had known his feet and hands were a mess, but he could not see his face and had not realized it was worthy of so much clucking. There was only a little pain, but it was starting to build. He looked for Janice, but she was not there.

The NP put some kind of plastic boots over his feet and one hand. His face had been bandaged and his arm had been poked with needles full of painkillers, antibiotics and clot busters. Chief Lawrence had been there the whole time. And so had Bearbait Bodette, stacking little boxes of bandages to create miniature walls and forts and bridges.

When the round-faced nurse was done clucking, Dewberry was rolled into another ambulance and taken all the way to the big hospital in Ashland. At every stop he told the story of his deliverance by spirit or spirits unknown. By a divine bear, maybe.

That story reached Grant at the speed of gossip, which is significantly faster than light. And the next morning he was up at Raspberry Bay, checking it out for himself.

Dewberry's car had been left where it was, which was good. But the ambulance and attendants had trampled a lot of snow in the vicinity.

The wind and light snow continued. But Dewberry's tracks, headed off toward the lake, were still faintly visible. As he had said, there were no tracks returning.

If he were a young man, or even a healthy old man, Grant would have made the trek to the lake. But probably he would have found nothing of interest. The hole in the ice would have frozen over, and the strong winds on the lake and blowing snow would have wiped everything clean.

Grant was about ready to leave when Sheriff Lewis Radisson drove up in his pickup, his uniform and gun belt covered by a heavy down parka.

"I knew you would be here," Lewis said. "Wherever a ghost goes, you'll be not far behind."

"How did you hear about this?"

"Jackie picked it up from a county ambulance driver."

"It's on the reservation."

"I'm not here to investigate. I'm just a tourist delivering a message. FBI Special Agent Benjamin Tuba is trying to get ahold of you."

"I shut off my phone. Too many telemarketers."

"Here is his card. Do you remember Tuba?"

"Sure. The FBI brings him in every time us redskins get out of line."

"Yeah. He's Navajo. But I guess in Washington, an Indian is an Indian."

"And the only good one is … well, you know. Is Tuba still breaking your balls?"

"Oh yeah. I have now been renamed Sheriff Lewis Inconsequential."

"Nice. What's he want with me?"

"A powwow, I guess. Maybe you two can smoke a pipe."

"Uh-huh."

"I figure if he's calling you for help, he's desperate."

Grant used his right hand to pull his right eyelid open so he could see Radisson clearly without the double vision. "He's dredging the bottom."

"He's full of crap, but you know him. He's one of the good ones. He hates being the redskin-on-call. Hates it. And really hates having to leave Arizona for sub-arctic Wisconsin."

"Poor thing."

"Pump him for information, will you? The feds don't tell me anything. How you feeling?"

"Better. On a one-to-ten scale, I've gone from one to one-point-two."

"Progress is progress. What did you find here? Is it like that tomahawk cop said? A big thunderbird plucked him out of the water and dropped him in his cruiser?"

"That's what it looks like."

"Maybe it's the same bird that got old man Weegwasi."

'Probably. But Weegwasi's bird left tracks. This one did not."

"Nothing?"

"Not a thing."

Radisson whistled. "Maybe the kid made it all up."

"What we have here is the trail of one man walking to the lake and nobody walking back."

"Well, Sam, that makes no sense."

"I'm not telling you what makes sense."

"You don't believe in this spirit thing, do you? I mean, not really."

"Lewis, until something better comes along, it's the best I've got."

"Well, something better will come along."

"I sure hope it does."

TWENTY-EIGHT

WHEN JACOB Dewberry woke up in his warm hospital bed, Grant was there watching. So was Benjamin Tuba, an enormous man with the shoulders of a linebacker but the waist of a ballerina. Dewberry looked them both over for a long time before he said, "Hi."

"Patrolman Dewberry, this is Special Agent Tuba of the FBI," Grant began. "He's Navajo."

"I can see."

"How are you feeling?" Grant asked.

"It's too early to tell. Wait until I get coffee."

"I've got some coming. I know the administrator here. We take care of each other. How are your feet?"

"They hurt. I hope I don't lose them."

"Hurting is a good thing. The doctor says you'll be fine."

"Did you hear what happened?"

"I heard."

"Do you think I'm crazy? Everyone else does."

"No, I don't, Jacob. But I think you are wrong. There has to be an explanation."

"I spent all night trying to think of one. Does Agent Tuba speak?"

"Like a magpie. Believe me. He's in his observation mode, but once he gets started you can't shut him up."

"Have you known him long?"

"Yeah. He's like the pinch Indian. He comes in when the white guys strike out."

"Have they struck out?"

"Yeah, I think so."

"We have a wrecked airplane with a Russian fashion plate we can't identify," Tuba finally said, his big voice suddenly filling the room. "No dope. No money. No witnesses. No explanation. We're hoping you can help us."

"Why me? I flunked out of high school."

"Because Mr. Grant here believes you know something you're not telling. And Mr. Grant has always been a good source."

"I don't know anything."

"You are a lousy liar, Officer Dewberry. You shouldn't even try. It's not in your nature. But let's pass over that for the moment. Let's deal with this *chindi* encounter of yours. A *chindi* is a Navajo ghost. I don't know what you forest injuns call them. They are made up of all the bad stuff that's left over when someone dies."

"*Wiindigoog.*"

"Whatever. We think so much of *chindis* down in New Mexico and Arizona that we named a town for them. How about that? But I've never seen one and don't expect to. I doubt you will either. So let's look at the evidence. Let me show you how I make my living. Would that be all right?"

"Sure," Dewberry said meekly.

"Then you can show me how you make your living. And the three of us red men can sit here and solve this whole thing and I can go home and lay in the sun."

"Okay."

Tuba got up, took Dewberry's hand and turned it over. "That's quite a bruise you have on your wrist."

"Got them all over. I was hitting the underside of the ice. Then I fell at the car."

"How is your shoulder?"

"It hurts."

"Let me show you something, Officer Dewberry. If I take off my belt, like this, and I run it through the buckle until there's just a little loop at the end. Then if I lay down spread-eagle on the ice to disburse my weight, and I wiggle up to you in your hole, all I have to do is slip this loop over your hand and pull it tight on your wrist. Like so."

Dewberry winched from the pain.

"Then I wiggle back until I'm as far away from the hole as I can get and still grab the end of the belt. Then I just start pulling. Maybe you break more ice as you come toward me, but I just keep backing up. Eventually you're going to hit good ice and I'm going to just slide you right up out of that lake. But I'm going to leave a hell of a bruise on your wrist. And your shoulder is going to hurt."

"I'll be darned," Dewberry said. So did Grant.

"It's a military technique taught in every Arctic survival school. So now look here. We just learned something. Your *chindi* has been in the army. What do you think about that?"

"How'd I get back to the car?"

"Well, you're not real big, but I'd hate to have to carry you a mile through old snow. So I told the doctor, I said, 'Let's figure he was in the lake for ten minutes.' I don't think you could have lived longer than that. And let's figure a big strong guy like me is going to need a half hour to get him to his car. I asked him, 'Is that enough time to get frostbit like that?' And you know what he said?"

"No," Dewberry said.

"That's right. That's exactly what he said. He said your injuries are consistent with what you'd expect if someone laid for three or four hours in wet clothes in freezing conditions."

"Wow."

"Yeah. So what's that tell you?"

"It tells me that whoever pulled me out was unsure what to do with me. Maybe he left. Maybe he went to get help."

"Keep going."

"Maybe he left to get something." Dewberry's eyes brightened. "Maybe he went home and got a toboggan or a snow boat. He pulled me back to the car on that, walking ahead, so that every step he took was erased by the sled."

"Bingo."

"The toboggan would have left just a little indentation in the hard snow, and the wind would have covered it by the time I looked. Besides, it was almost dark."

"You're a good man, Officer Dewberry. A good Indian, as they say. Smart as a whip, dropout or no. Now tell me what we got."

"We have a man who was watching me for some reason. We don't know why. He was hiding so well I didn't know he was there. He saw me fall and moved quickly to save me. So he cared enough about me to give me a chance. But he didn't care enough to call an ambulance for me or stay around to help. He didn't want to be identified. Again, we don't know why. He lives somewhere in the area. He's been in the army. He's gone to cold weather survival school. He has a toboggan ... and a very handy belt."

Agent Tuba grinned. "Well, well, well. Mr. Grant, we got a winner here, just like you said. Picks right up on things. And he's thorough. I might take him back to Arizona."

"But what about the bear? I didn't see a man, just a bear."

"Hallucination, maybe. I can't explain the bear."

"I don't think so."

"You were drowning. You were short of air. Your mind could have played tricks."

"There was a bear."

"Jacob," Grant said, "that plane crash is a problem. It has caught the attention of a lot of white people who wear suits and work in big cities, and that is never a good thing for us."

"No, it is not," Tuba agreed. "Jacob, I am pretty sure you know exactly what happened with that plane crash. And why."

"Yes."

"But you don't want to tell us."

"No, sir. I don't."

Grant looked at Dewberry and suddenly realized why he had so liked this young officer's spirit, what he had sensed from the beginning. Dewberry was a very young man, and vulnerable to the same insecurities as other young men. But there was a wholeness to him that was unusual. Everything he needed was already inside him. He wasn't going to show off. He didn't need reinforcement. Dewberry would play the game the way he wanted to play it. Or not at all.

TWENTY-NINE

AFTER COFFEE they had breakfast together, brought in on big round trays, not the little square hospital trays. Jacob sat up and hung his feet off the side of the bed, but did not try to stand. Even the act of dangling his feet seemed to cause pain. He was attached to a drip and limited by its short tube.

"Apparently, the risk is infection," he explained. "Don't want to get gangrene."

Tuba avoided business talk. He was just trying to get to know the young man now, to develop a relationship. He was in no hurry. There was nothing on his schedule he needed to do. He was sure this bright young high school dropout held all the keys.

Somehow the conversation had turned to the Catholic Church, and Dewberry was ranting about Pope Alexander VI and the papal bull he issued in 1493.

"What he said was that no land was owned until it was owned by a Christian," Dewberry said. "As a result, that's what Columbus believed, and all those who came later. We Indians were pagans and therefore could not actually own land. It was theirs for the taking. It was their religious duty."

"You read a lot of history, huh?" Grant asked.

"Yes, sir."

"White folks have always made their own rules," Grant said. "Everywhere they've gone. Now they say we're warming the climate and everyone has to stop doing what they've been doing. What the hell? Global warming is a white problem. It's caused by white people. Can't they see that? How much warming do you suppose is caused by African villagers? How much by Navajo and Ojibwe? How much? The world just got too white, and now it is coming to get us."

"We're lucky to have anything left," Dewberry said. "I grew up at Lac Court Oreilles. It's a beautiful reservation but pretty small. Red Cliff is even smaller."

"What you have is a bunch of tiny little islands of your people scattered here and yon," Tuba said. "Your reservations are scenic. But the *bilagaana* scattered you out like that so you couldn't work together. *Bilagaana* is what we Navajos call white people. What do you call them?"

"*Wayaabishkiiwed*, in the old language," Grant said.

"But most of us just call them *joganosh,*" Dewberry said. "It's not quite as nice. It comes from the expression 'long knives'."

"Perfect! Then by God, we'll call them *joganosh,*" Tuba bellowed. "No need to be polite here. They are burning down the whole damn planet. Anyway, us Navajo were allowed to stay together on our sacred land, but it's not very pretty. Well, it's pretty enough, but it's dry. You know what I mean? We got to stay together because the white people, frankly, didn't want that land. But that was their mistake; 170,000 of us now live on one reservation. It's a big part of four states. We got muscle. We got clout.

"What you Ojibwe have is lots of casinos in lots of pretty places. But you got no muscle. You got the biggest Indian nation in North America, bigger even than the Navajo, but you're scatted all over two countries.

"In 125 independent bands," Grant said.

"Yeah, that's what I mean. Nobody cares about you. You are marginalized because you're so fractured. If you asked the average *bilagaana* in Arizona how many Navajo he thought there were, he'd say about ten million. That's because we make so much noise. But you ask the average *joganosh* here in Wisconsin how many Ojibwe there are and he's gonna say five, maybe six. See what I mean? You don't make enough noise. How many cops you got at Red Cliff?"

"Police chief, a sergeant and four patrolmen," Dewberry said.

"That's what I mean. When something happens at your place, all us feds come in and walk all over you. We pat you on the head and shoo you away like little puppies. What can you do? Your whole police force can fit in a taxi. In Arizona we got 200 Navajo cops. Agents like me have to be careful there. We have to be respectful. We have to share a little bit of information."

Grant nodded. "Nicely done, Agent Tuba. You have just steered the conversation where you wanted it to go."

"That's right. Information sharing. And now that's just what we're going to do. You notice I said *sharing*. Now the average FBI agent is going to come here and demand to know everything you know, like he has a right to do that. And he's not going to tell you anything he knows. Like you have no right to know. Well, I'm not like that. So, here's what I'm going to do. I'm going to lay out for you everything I know. Every little thing. I'm going to talk solid for like the next half hour, because I like to do that. And when I am done, I hope you will join me in this exercise of sharing.

"We got a ski plane flew in here illegally from Canada without calling customs. It tried to land on a little bay in Red Cliff, but it cracked up and killed the passenger, who we will call the Russian because he was wearing clothes custom-made in Moscow. The pilot, who we will call the Canadian, survived but was seriously injured. He was, subsequent to the crash, dispatched by a nasty blow to his head. He was bleeding for about an hour before he was killed."

"Now that plane was in perfect condition. It did not make an emergency landing. It flew in here for a reason, and any reason you can think of requires someone on the ground waiting for it. We'll call that someone the host. Maybe it was bringing in dope. Maybe it was bringing in money. Or maybe it was picking up one or the other. Or both. We found nothing in the plane, not even a trace of dope. And no odor a dog could pick up.

"Now the plane could have just been bringing in the Russian, to drop him off, to avoid customs. But there was no baggage on the plane, and he sure wasn't dressed like someone who expected to go unnoticed in the Wisconsin sticks.

"Now the host was probably unhappy that plane crashed. Maybe he got mad and killed the pilot. Maybe he just wanted to be sure the pilot wouldn't talk. But why did he wait almost an hour to do it?

"If the plane was carrying something of value, the host made off with it. Both doors had been pried open.

But the host left no clues. Not so much as a fingerprint or a fiber or a hair. The Russian had no wallet or anything that would identify him.

"Now I probably haven't told you anything much you didn't already surmise. But I'm not done. The Russian passenger in the nice suit has no fingerprints or DNA on file in the U.S. So he's not your ordinary Russian mafia guy. He's probably a Russian national who does not often come to the New World. We are trying to do a facial recognition, but he was pretty smashed up.

"Now when you check international flights coming into Canada in the days preceding the crash, you find a shocking number of Russians. Shocking. I mean, what's the story? Can't they get enough winter in Moscow? I had no idea there was so much business interaction between the Canucks and the Soviets. And my God, the hockey players. Anyway, there is one guy who flew into Toronto two days before the crash. Alexander Dubcek. You ever hear of him?"

Grant and Dewberry shook their heads.

"He's one of those millionaire Russkies connected to the top guy, an oligarch who runs rackets all over the world. We don't have his prints because he has never been to the U.S., as far as we know. He is one of those guys the treasury has sanctioned for bad behavior, and to annoy his buddy Putin. That means we've seized all his bank accounts and generally made it hard for him to do business in dollars. He, of course, would never be allowed in the U.S. And he'd be arrested if we caught him. But he's safe in Canada and has been flying in about every three months. Interesting, huh? There's no record of him taking commercial flights to anywhere else in

Canada, like Thunder Bay. But he could charter a plane for that. Or drive.

"If that's him on the plane, and we'll know sooner or later, that's really good news. Happy to be rid of him. But it makes that plane trip more interesting, not less. So we're getting a lot of heat from the top. Treasury wants to know what he was doing here, who he was meeting and so forth. And, of course, we know squat.

"Now that's where Officer Dewberry here comes in. He has apparently passed on to Samuel Grant a broken part from a snowmobile, said part having been found by Officer Dewberry as the result of a thorough search through the snow in the vicinity of the airplane. Of course, Officer Dewberry has filed no report on this event, and it is entirely confidential.

"Now I gather that Officer Dewberry is thinking there might have been a snowmobile on that bay, buried in the snow. Maybe it broke down in a snowstorm and the owner left it. But the pilot didn't see it and tripped over it when his skis sank down on landing.

"Now this notion gets interesting when one considers that the snowmobile was not there when our people arrived. That means the owner removed it after the accident but before the first responders came. Therefore, that owner—we will call him the mystery man—may have been witness to many unusual things. That is a development which one can only describe as electrifying, considering how little else we have to go on. The fact that a mystery man was very recently surveilling that crash site, and was therefore on hand to rescue our hero when he fell though the ice, lends credence to all this. And the fact he didn't call an ambulance or hang around to be identified tells me he knows something and is probably scared."

Tuba was studying Dewberry to gauge his reaction, but the youthful face gave away nothing.

"Now we can be pretty sure that snowmobiler was Ojibwe or he would have been trespassing. And we can be sure he has a broken throttle lever. Shouldn't be hard to find." Tuba looked at Dewberry and raised his eyebrows. "Unless there is some reason we shouldn't go looking for him. A reason that might explain why our hero has put none of this into a report."

There was a long silence while Grant and Tuba looked at Dewberry, who kept his head down and his expression locked.

"Well. What do you have to share, Officer Dewberry?"

"There are about 2,500 Ojibwe on the reservation at any given time," the young patrolman said softly. "And every one of them has a snowmobile, half of them broken."

"But you could find this one, couldn't you? The mystery man. The witness. The one with the broken throttle lever."

"Sure," Dewberry said.

"Will you do that for us, Officer Dewberry?"

"No, sir."

Tuba sighed deeply and looked at Grant. "He is just what you said."

"I told you. He has his own agenda. If he won't talk, he won't talk."

Grant turned to Dewberry and spoke softly. "Jacob, this is *joganosh* stuff. It doesn't concern us."

"It does," Dewberry replied. He lifted his head and looked Tuba square in the eyes. "There was not one snowmobile. There were at least ten, maybe twelve, in a perfect line across the bay. Spaced about ten feet apart. They were brought in after the first storm. They were buried by the second and removed after the crash."

"And our people never noticed that?" Tuba asked.

"The top layer of snow was covered with drifts. You couldn't see anything. You had to dig down to the deeper layers, with a trowel, to see what happened. The snowmobile tracks were clear, but about five feet down."

There followed a long period of stunned silence. Grant and Tuba looked at each other, both bewildered.

"There were no fingerprints because it was like a hundred below on that lake in the wind," Dewberry said. The baby-faced dropout sensed that he had just taken command. "Everyone would have been in heavy gloves, parkas and wool caps. And nobody was waiting for the plane on that lake. It would have been suicide. The host was waiting someplace warm, and came only after he spotted the plane flying over or was signaled. By the time he got to the bay and snowshoed in, it would have been an hour. Killing that pilot was probably the first thing he did."

"Well, crap," Tuba said. "Now I got to start all over. Did the host put those snowmobiles there to intentionally wreck the plane?"

"Almost impossible," Grant said. "Logistically, you just can't bring that many snowmobiles into Red Creek without a lot of people noticing. Anyway, there was no way to predict that second storm would hide the machines. I think the machines were put there to block the airplane, to keep it from landing. But after the second storm, the pilot couldn't see them."

"So here's the big question," Tuba said. "The guys with the snowmobiles. When did they get there? Before or after the hosts arrived?"

"Before," Dewberry said without hesitation.

"How can you know that?"

"Because they had taken what the plane carried. A case of some kind. Metal." Jacob told the story of the dark-eyed man with the big pistol and the heavy accent.

"Well, I'll be damned." Tuba said. "The snowmobile guys got the goods before the hosts arrived. I just went from zero witnesses to ten or twelve. The trouble is, how do I find those witnesses, living as they do, on a reservation, which is essentially another country?"

The men just looked at each other for a long time.

"Who killed the pilot?" Tuba wondered.

"The hosts," Grant said. "And they took all the passenger's ID. They got there too late, and they were unhappy."

Grant looked at Dewberry and nodded and smiled. "I understand now, Jacob. I understand everything."

"I don't," Tuba said. "But I don't imagine that either one of you really cares about that."

"Agent Tuba," Grant said, looking suddenly very serious, "let us handle it from here. Will you do that? It's Ojibwe business. You and your friends will just blunder around and make it harder."

There was a long silence as Tuba looked from one man to the other. Finally he said, "Bring me that case. That's all I want. I don't care about anything else. Bring me the case and we will all be big heroes. All three of us. But I have to have the case."

"We'll try," Grant said. "I think we can. But if it was full of money, the money is long gone."

"Just get me the case. If it can identify the passenger, it must contain something we'll be very, very interested in. Meanwhile, I'll just twiddle my thumbs, I guess." Tuba demonstrated. "I'm not very good at it. Maybe I'll start knitting."

Dewberry picked up a paper and pencil and wrote down an Illinois license plate number. "Why don't you hunt this down? It's the dark-eyed man who was looking for the case."

"I thought he took your dash cam," Tuba said.

"He did. But I keep another camera pointed backward. It caught him as he left."

Tuba laughed for a short time, paused for a minute, looked at the number, pondered something, and then laughed for a very long time ... laughed so hard everyone else had to start laughing, too. Even the nurses who stuck their heads in the door would laugh.

"Remarkable," the agent finally said. "I bet you filmed this whole interview."

"No, sir, Dewberry said, pointing to his phone on the table. "I recorded it."

"You were sleeping when we came in," Grant said.

"Yes, sir. I recorded all night. I like to know what happens when I'm asleep."

Tuba laughed again. "Mr. Grant, this young man is going places. I doubt he ever needed us."

THIRTY

T HE NEXT DAY Grant drove to Walmart in Ashland and parked where he knew the cell signal was good. He shut off the engine, took a deep breath, and called his wife.

Jeannie seemed reluctant to talk, but Grant did his best to be positive. The first thing she asked was, "How is the new house?"

"Oh, the new house," he said. "Well, it needs a little work right now."

"I hope you didn't spend a lot of money on it … you know … hoping I would come."

"I've given up on that," he said.

"Good. I'm happy here, Sam. I'm a Chicago high-rise kind of woman, I guess. I know you're not. There are many things I miss. I think about you all the time. But I have moved on."

"I know. I've given up on … on pretty much everything."

"How is your health?"

"I got my vaccinations. I'm good as gold. I hid pretty well and that virus never found me. How about you?"

"I'm good. Also vaccinated. I meant your leg and your hand. You know, the trouble you were having when you stopped by here after Paraguay."

"All healed," Grant said.

"Really? Because you don't sound just right. You sound like you're having trouble talking."

"I'm in my truck with the heater off. I guess I'm a little cold."

"Really?"

"I got worse for a while, but I'm on the mend. I'm actually working for the sheriff again. And I was walking for exercise, but there's been so much snow lately."

"Here too. Sam, why did you call? Do you want something?"

"It's a little hard to explain. My work recently carried me into the home of someone who was grieving something awful. It reminded me of … of so many things. I don't have to mention them."

"No. Please."

"So I've been thinking a lot about grief, and how it changes people, and how there is no going back to the people you were before. What we went through isn't something you ever get past because it isn't ever really over. And I know now that I have been wanting something that is not possible. I have been wanting to go back, and we can't do that."

"No."

"I had this need to … to finish what we started. To finish the marriage. Do you understand?"

"The marriage is finished, Sam. I wish you could see that."

"Oh, I do, Jeannie. And I understand now it was wrong to try. It didn't finish the way I wanted it to, but nothing does."

"Do you want a divorce?"

"No, ma'am. I want something much smaller."

"What?"

"A few days of your time. This summer. Let's meet in Gatlinburg, like the old days. Let's tour the Smokeys and go to a few bars. Hang out a little."

"Oh, Sam. You're crazy."

"Branson. Take in some shows."

"Sam."

"Galena. Do some antiquing. Go to General Grant's house again. Stay at that really nice place with the view."

"Galena."

"We could both drive there. You wouldn't even have to leave the state. Lots of good memories in that town."

"I'd like to see Galena again. Such a nice old town."

"Me too."

"I am dying to do something. I feel so caged up by this epidemic."

"Me too."

"Galena. Then what, Sam? What comes next?"

"Nothing. Absolutely nothing. You go back to your life. I go back to … I go back."

"Really? No strings?"

"No strings. Jeannie, I understand now that I have been asking too much of you, and too much of me. You can't give up your life and I can't give up mine. When I bought the home in Ashland, I thought I was finding someplace in the middle. But there is no middle. Any place in the middle is home to neither of us."

"That's right."

"But you are still my best friend. You are the only one left who knew me when I was a young man. And I knew you when you were a hot young woman. We had some great times together."

"Yes, we did."

"Let's not lose those memories, along with everything else. Let's celebrate them, have a toast to them. What do you say?"

"I'd go to Galena for a weekend. That sounds really fun. But Sam, can you walk? Truly? There's nothing to do there but walk."

"Jeannie, when I get to Galena, I will walk. I will run. I will dance."

After the call, Sam looked up at the store, and then looked for a parking place that would be closer. He had promised to bring back some meat and bread for Mrs. Brebeuf, but he could just tell her he forgot.

He slid out the door and held on to the front fender until he was sure he had his balance. Then he started limping toward the nearest shopping cart he could see. He figured that once he got that cart for support, he could make it to the bakery section, and maybe even the meat case. The milk and eggs would be all the way in back, and probably out of reach.

Galena, he thought. With Jeannie. He smiled and nodded. It was enough to keep him going for a while longer. Just a while.

A reporter understands that every story ends in death, and if it does not end in death, it is because you stopped the story before it could get there. Grant had stopped many stories when they were at the top, when they were fun and happy and made the reader feel good. The trouble is, you cannot stop your own.

THIRTY-ONE

W HEN GRANT got back to the truck, with two loaves of bread and nothing else, he phoned Radisson to fill him in on the meeting with Tuba.

"A case," Radisson said. "What sort of a case?"

"I don't know."

"Drugs?"

"Maybe."

"Money?"

"Don't know."

"Where is it?"

"There's only one place it can be," Grant said. "Who else can mount an operation like that? A dozen snowmobiles lined up to block a plane from landing."

"You tell me."

"The Bear Clan. That plane had probably been coming on a regular schedule. The clan put their machines across the bay to tell the drug smugglers they knew what was going on and wouldn't allow it. But then the storm blew in and the plane didn't come on schedule. Instead, the snowmobiles were buried. My guess is the clan guys were just on their way to pick up their machines when the plane came in."

"And they took the case?"

"Why not?"

"How are you going to get it? You going up there? That's a rough neighborhood."

"It's my family, Lewis. It's my dad, probably. What could happen?"

"You could get shot and fed to the dogs."

"I mean, besides that."

"I better go along."

"Not a chance. I'm taking Jacob Dewberry."

"I think you should take someone a little, well, bigger."

"No, he's perfect. We'll go up on his day off, without his gun. He's new. He should meet Standing Bear and Nathan Boudreaux. And the whole clan."

"You'll have to go in there on snowmobiles. You'll never get your truck into that place. Are you up for that? I mean physically?"

"We'll find out."

"Takes some gifts. You know, food. They'll probably appreciate that."

"Maybe beads, huh? Little mirrors?"

"I'm serious. It's been a long winter."

"Wine will do for my dad. They eat venison in the winter. They're fine."

"Okay. It's your neck. But I really don't think you should take Dewberry."

"Why not?"

"Sam, I'm not sure I can tell you."

"Then I'm taking him."

"Listen, Sam. You have an interesting theory, and maybe you are right. But there's another theory out there, and it involves Dewberry."

"I don't believe that."

"I haven't talked to Tuba. He doesn't much like me. But I've had another FBI agent in here three times, quizzing me about Dewberry and you."

"Me?"

"Yes, and I have assured him that you are not mentally capable of committing a crime."

"Well, thanks for that."

"Unless, of course, you're faking this whole stroke business."

"Did you tell him that?"

"I'm telling YOU that. Sam, I've known you for a long time. And I like you better than anyone else on this planet. But I never know what you're up to."

"I'm not faking anything."

"How about Dewberry? You see, because there is another organization that could have put those snowmobiles out there. The Red Cliff Tribal Police Department."

"That's crazy."

"They were first on the scene."

"They were closest."

"The FBI has an informant, Sam. Some Russian enforcer who would rather talk than be deported. They found him because Dewberry had his license number."

"I know about that."

"This informant says that his boss received several emails from someone claiming to be a federal agent, someone who says he has the case and will return it for $500,000."

"And they don't believe it's a federal agent."

"Of course not. They're not going to finger one of their own people. It's bad press."

"Dewberry is not involved."

"Sam, when the FBI ran this guy's license plate number, they discovered it had been run two days earlier … by a Red Cliff tribal policeman."

"Uh-oh."

"Sam, this Dewberry guy could have tracked down the enforcer and his boss just as easily as the feds."

"Maybe."

"Why did he give Tuba the license number when he already had the man's identity?"

"I don't know," Sam said. "I admit it looks bad."

"It makes sense, Sam. He's been out there digging around several times. He probably found the case. He's a young guy with no resources. That $500,000 would set him up for years. It would make his mark on this world."

"He's not the type."

"Retribution then. Against the guy who put his gun to Dewberry's head."

"Can't see it."

"Are you sure?"

"Well, not exactly. He has a complicated spirit."

"Do not go up there with him. It's dangerous and it makes you look guilty, too … like you're shifting the attention away from the police and onto the Bear Clan."

"It's too late. I'm going with Dewberry. It's all set."

Radisson heaved a deep sigh. "I sure hope you are telling me the truth, Sam. And that you're doing things smart this time. That's not your history."

"I know. I'm paying the price for my history."

"Well, listen. I have something else for you. We got the results back on the blood samples. It's pretty shocking."

"Really?"

"It's negative for Charlie Weegwasi. That was not him in that scrape. Some of it was wolf blood, of course. The rest belonged to an unidentified human, unrelated to Charlie in any way."

"Really."

"Yup. It blows everything I've worked on. There's nothing left to do. I erased my whole board."

"Case closed?"

"Charlie got scared by Bird Feet and ran off into the coldest night of the year. It's been a week. He's not coming back. That same night, Bird Feet got chased down by wolves. End of story. The victim and the perpetrator are both under the snow somewhere, probably in pieces. I hope next spring there's enough left of Bird Feet to identify him. I'd like to know who he was."

"I don't think you'll ever know."

"Nope. Isn't that something, Sam? The damn wolves ate my perp. Where else but Wisconsin, huh?"

Grant thought about that for a long time. "Lewis, I'll let you know how things go with the Bear Clan."

"I don't think you should go."

"I'll be fine."

"Sam, I admire your pluck, but my friend, unless you are faking, you cannot even tie your shoelaces."

Grant looked down at his untied laces, but that made him dizzy and he had to look up again. He cleared his throat. "No," he said. "I cannot. I am blind, lame and forgetful. But I have one thing left."

"What's that?"

"Uh … "

"What's that, Sam?"

"Lewis, I forgot."

THIRTY-TWO

AT FIRST LIGHT, Dewberry was up and loading two police snowcats on the department trailer. Bearbait Bodette was helping, cheerful as always. Both were dressed in jeans under snowmobile suits. It was their day off.

Dewberry's feet and hands were still sensitive to the cold, but he could walk, awkwardly, and even his worst hand could grip the handle and push the throttle. Probably.

It was a Sunday and nobody was around the tribal office or the department headquarters. Sensible people were in bed. But Sam Grant had asked for this favor, and what could he say? Sam had visited him every day in the hospital, bringing him little homemade potions that terrified the nurses but really helped the pain. His care and concern were pretty impressive, considering Chief Lawrence had come just once and Janice not at all.

But Janice had called twice from Eau Claire, where she had gone back for clinicals or labs or something. It wasn't clear to Dewberry what she was doing, exactly, but it was becoming clear that their very different lives would continue to throw thorns onto any path they tried to walk.

"Maybe we can get together this summer," she had said casually, perhaps not understanding that such a statement to a love-starved and sexually deprived young man in his prime was very much like a quick stab through the heart with a rusty butcher knife.

It wasn't that Dewberry couldn't wait until summer to get this relationship off the launchpad. He could. And for Janice, he would. It was just the lack of urgency in her manner. There was nothing honest he could say to her without appearing desperate, because desperate is exactly what he was. It was the damn kiss that did it.

Finished outside, Dewberry and Bodette sat in the small lunchroom, their feet on the table. Bearbait was playing some kind of game on his phone and periodically laughing. Dewberry was eating peanuts from the vending machine and contemplating that kiss for about the millionth time.

My God, what a kiss. He didn't know a mouth could feel so soft and supple, so luscious. And he had no idea that it would so quicken her breathing, so inflame her passion, that just a couple of kisses later she would be straddling his lap, her knees on the car seat, her butt against the steering wheel.

She would have both hands behind his head and would be pulling his mouth to hers so hard he was afraid she would break a tooth.

Then, just like that, it would be over. She would swing around and take her seat, clear her throat, straighten her scrubs and continue their last conversation without a single gap in the sentence she had just begun before the first kiss.

My God. What a remarkable introduction to Janice Newman's inner fire. In a matter of a few minutes, she had set ablaze all his plans of going slowly. She had thrown his caution into the ash bin and turned him into a human geyser, a molten hunk of insensible and unsatisfied desperation. Then, before he could even tell her how he felt, she was talking about getting together next summer. Maybe. Depending on COVID and the vaccinations and whatever else.

"It's just such a bad time," she had said. "Finals at school and so much work at the clinic." She would be in Eau Claire most of the spring, and when she was back in Red Cliff it would be on a seven-day schedule. After that, she was going to a hospital in Bismarck for a month.

He had figured she would at least have the summer free, but oh no. "I'm sorry," she said. "Didn't I tell you? I'm moving right into a master's program, and I start in June. I want to be a nurse practitioner."

It was a small police department, and the turnover in the vending machine was insufficient to guarantee any fresh product. He was sure these peanuts had been packed before World War II, but he didn't care. Anything was acceptable if, even for a moment, it took his mind off Janice Newman and those perfect pink lips.

Sam Grant had arrived and was fumbling with the trailer hitch, trying to get it on his truck. "Let me help," Dewberry said, rushing out the door in a very rapid limp.

"You're walking better than me already. I told you."

"I had first-class medicine, both old and new. I asked Officer Bodette to come along, if you don't mind. You and I are both pretty beat up. I thought it would be a good idea to have one good body along."

"Good idea."

"Where are we going? To the bay?"

"Nope. We're going to meet the man who saved your life. I thought you would want to say thank you."

"Are you kidding me? How did you find him? Who is he?"

"I have no idea."

Dewberry finished the hitch and all three climbed into Grant's truck, with Dewberry driving. "I never know what to think of you," the young officer said.

"Some things you just have to take by faith," Grant said. "Wow. I never thought anyone would ever hear me say that."

"I have to know where to drive."

"The Bear Clan compound. Do you know where that is?"

"I know generally. They usually have the drive blocked with a couple of old cars. And they have guards. I've never tried to go past that."

"The drive is a couple of miles long and they never plow it. Snowcats are the only way in. But I'm afraid I'm going to have to ride behind you. I can't drive."

"That's okay. Why are we going there?"

"I think you know."

"Yeah."

"Only the Bear Clan could organize an operation like that, putting a dozen snow machines across the bay and then keeping it under surveillance. You knew who did it as soon you saw what they had done."

"If the feds found out, they'd go blundering into that place. There could be a war. People would get hurt. I couldn't let that happen. I had to make a choice, and I made one."

"You made the right one, Jacob. And you made it with very little knowledge of the people involved. You made it instinctively. That's the best way. It's time for you to meet the people."

"I struggled with the knowledge."

"The tribe is family, Jacob. It's your family. It's not perfect. We have drunks and gamblers and dopers. We have wife abusers and a few bad parents. But it's our family. It's what we have left when everything else is gone. Do you understand?"

"Sure."

"The Bear Clan raises hell sometimes, and sometimes it's embarrassing. But in a pinch, there are no people I'd rather have watching my back. Or watching your back."

"Do you think the guy who saved my life will be there?"

"It's Sunday, so there's a good chance."

"Tell me what we're going to find."

"Well, there will be guards. We'll have to deal with that. Up the drive is a collection of four or five frame houses and that many more trailer homes. The biggest house belongs to Standing Bear. He runs everything; he has for decades. He comes out of the Indian protest movement back in the '60's. He served time and was brutalized in prison because he is so big. He's a formidable man, even at his age. But I'm bringing him a gift." Grant winked. "He loves French Chablis.

"The house next to his belongs to Nathan Boudreaux. He's married and has a couple of kids. Nathan is a real solid guy. He served in the Tenth

Mountain Division and is, among other things, a sniper and an explosives expert. He would be the most dangerous guy in the clan except that he is the most stable. He's helped me out on many occasions.

"While Bear is still a protester at heart, Nathan is an operations guy. I figure the snowcat thing on the bay was Bear's idea. Nathan would have done it better. I'm betting the bay was watched constantly after the crash. That would have been Nathan's work. That's why you're alive today."

"You think he's the one who saved me?"

"We'll find out. He's the one who would have known the technique used. Nathan is forty years younger than Bear, but still older than all the others. He'll almost certainly take over when the Bear is gone.

"There will be about a dozen to fifteen other young bucks around. Most of them have wives or girlfriends there, and lots of dogs. Big dogs."

"I've met one."

"Some of the women are pretty formidable, too. They all have a lot of guns.

"Outside the compound, scattered around the reservation, are what I'd call the short list: about fifty clan members who will come on a moment's notice, armed and ready. A lot of them are paid by Bear to do repairs and yard work and operate his gravel pits. He has, I think, three pits within fifty miles and sells to both the tribe and the county. He must be making a fortune, considering all the flooding roads.

"Then there's the long list: other clan members who are available but not often on call. At least a hundred of those. Maybe 150. How many officers did you say you had?"

"Five."

"And that, my friend, is why we are going there today. Bear is kind of a godfather. If someone needs money or a job, he'll fix them up. He'll make one call and the next day they'll be working at the casino or driving a snowplow or working on the tribal road crew."

"I've heard a lot about him."

"He is a good friend to have. Or a bad enemy. But his primary concern is the welfare of the tribe, and as long as that's your primary concern, the two of you can work things out."

"Is it true he's your father?"

"Probably. I guess he and my mother were pretty close for a while. He and my grandmother, too."

"And she was a shaman? That's what people say."

"She was a remarkable person, kind and wise and just crammed with knowledge. She was the biggest influence in my life while she was alive. And pretty much still is. For many years I have felt her presence in my life, for good and bad. It's hard to explain. I have not felt her for many months, but I do again today. I don't know why. Perhaps because I am visiting my father—something I have neglected."

They drove as far as they could and pulled off. Sam's big truck could have gone father in the deepening snow, but not the trailer. It was another half an hour, on the two snowmobiles, before they reached the junction with the drive that led back to the Bear Clan compound. Grant rode behind Dewberry on one of the machines, and Bodette rode the other.

Blocking the road was an old car of some sort. It was impossible to tell what because it was buried up to the bottom of the windows in snow. A rug-size area had been dug out by one side so the passenger door could be swung open. Inside was a young man, maybe eighteen or nineteen, with long black hair and the kind of attitude you get when you've been sitting in a cold car in a snowbank for several hours. Grant hoped he would recognize the guard, but he didn't.

"Closed," the guard said, getting out and standing up. "Private property."

"Oh, I know. I've been here many times. I'm Sam Grant. Do you recognize me?"

"The mask," the young man growled.

"Oh, of course, sorry." Grant stood up and approached the guard, removing his mask and smiling. "Standing Bear is my father."

"I don't know you."

"Yeah. It's been a while."

"Did he ask you to come?"

"No," Grant admitted. "But I'm bringing him a gift."

"Come back tomorrow. I'll ask him tonight."

"Can't you just call him now?" Dewberry asked, getting up and coming over. "I'm working tomorrow."

The young man looked at Dewberry like he was stupid, and Grant put his hand up to tell Jacob to back off.

Smiling at the young guard, Sam said, "I'll tell you what … what did you say your name was?"

"I didn't say."

"Yeah. Okay then. We'll just call you Stranded, Mr. Stranded. Because since your snowcat won't start, you'll have to walk two miles through the snow."

"My Polaris is fine."

"It's dead as a doornail. I've got twenty dollars that says it won't start. Try it. If it starts, the money is yours." Grant held up the bill.

The guard sniffed, took two steps and threw his leg over the machine. He turned his head back to watch Grant while he pressed the starter button, but the machine didn't make a sound. The boy's expression turned to one of concern. He tried again and then again.

"Battery must be down," he murmured.

"Sure," Grant said.

The boy adjusted the choke then pulled the recoil starter. Then he pulled it again, holding the rope all the way out. Then again and again.

Grant, Dewberry, and Bearbait got back on their snowcats, started them, and pulled up next to the guard. "We'll find Nathan Boudreaux and tell him you need help out here," Grant shouted over the noise of the engine. "You try to stay warm."

A mile down the drive, Jacob released his throttle and let the machine come to a stop. He turned on his seat to look at Grant. "What was that all about? Did you do something?"

"No, no. That was Grandma." Grant smiled. "She doesn't like mechanical things, and she *really* doesn't like boys who do not respect their elders."

"Your grandmother is dead."

"Yup," Grant said, nodding. "Good thing for him, too. You should have seen her when she was alive."

THIRTY-THREE

GRANT POINTED and motioned for Dewberry to stop next to a stocky man in a heavy green coat. The sleeves had dingy shadows where once there had been stripes. The coat was old and dirty.

"My friend Nathan Boudreaux," Grant gushed, pulling his mask down again to show his face. "How are you?"

People were coming out of their houses and trailers and lumbering through the snow toward the new arrivals. Some had guns. All had dogs, and the people yelled and cursed trying to keep them in control.

"Better than you," Nathan answered. "What happened to your eye?"

"It's a long story," Grant sighed, standing up. "I had a little mix-up in Paraguay. I haven't fully recovered yet." Nathan was holding a two-way radio, and Grant knew the guard had called him. "I told Mr. Stranded up the road there I'd tell you his predicament."

"He said his Polaris would not start."

"Bad luck, huh?"

"He said you just ran on by. He could have shot you."

"Naw. His gun wouldn't have worked either."

"What are you up to, Grant?"

"I just came to introduce my new friends here, Jacob Dewberry and Bearbait Bodette. And have a little chat with Standing Bear about a missing case of some sort, a metal one."

Nathan looked at Dewberry with narrowed eyes. "This is the new cop. He shouldn't be here. You either. He is not Bear Clan, and you should not have brought him here. The other one is okay. He's clan."

"You're Bear Clan?" Grant asked, turning to Bearbait.

"I think so," he said with a shrug.

"Nathan, I think you and Jacob Dewberry are going to be good friends. He just wants to find the guy who saved his life at the bay and say thank you."

Dewberry got up off the machine and tried to smile into the scowl on Boudreaux's face. "Hi," he said. "Glad to meet you." Nathan continued to look him over and finally Dewberry added, "I wouldn't be here today if you hadn't saved me."

Nathan grunted. "It was Sidney." With the radio and its antennae, he pointed toward a young man coming their way.

"Do you mind if I go say hello?"

Nathan grunted again, and Dewberry left them to go meet Sidney.

"I thought it might have been you," Grant said softly, watching Dewberry walk away. "The rescuer used a technique the army teaches in cold weather training."

"Sidney saw him fall and called me. I told him what to do."

Grant nodded. "Of course. Thank you."

"I had nothing to do with any of that plane business."

"I know that, Nathan. I already told Dewberry that very thing. You would have done it a lot better. You organized the surveillance afterward, though. You kept your eye on that bay."

"There were cops and agents of every sort."

"Uh-huh."

"My people are on edge. You should not have come or brought the cops."

"Well, it was going to be just a friendly visit. But my grandmother just took over a couple of miles back. She hasn't been with me for months, and now all of a sudden she's in a snit. I don't think she's happy with the Bear."

"It was stupid," Nathan said.

"They might have been bringing in dope on that plane."

"They weren't. The plane was flying in the first Monday every three months, so Bear thought it was dope."

Grant nodded. "So he organized a protest, just like he's always done. He put out a perfect line of snowmobiles to warn those people away. It makes sense, from his standpoint. But the storm came in and delayed the plane and buried the machines. Am I right?"

"The storm was forecast."

"I'm not saying it wasn't a mistake."

"This young cop could tell someone."

"Nathan, this young cop figured it out way before the rest of us, and he told no one."

Nathan nodded. "I thought that might be true. He always came to the bay alone. Maybe we can trust him."

"I brought the Bear a bottle of wine."

"He's been drinking all day."

"Well, that's not going to make this any easier."

"He's in his house watching TV. Good luck. When you leave, help Jeremy start his snowmobile."

"Jeremy? That's the guard?"

Nathan sniffed. "Some guard."

THIRTY-FOUR

SAM GRANT knocked on the door out of customary courtesy, then just went in. Standing Bear would never have been able to hear the knock, and even if he had, he wouldn't have answered. So there wasn't much point.

There was a smoky fire in the old brick fireplace, and the curtains were all closed. No lights were on. The dingy room was lit only by the big TV screen that flickered off the faded wallpaper and ceiling. Bear was watching a ten-year-old rerun of a detective show set in Hawaii or Florida or someplace warm, with palms trees. For sure, it was not set in Wisconsin.

The huge old man sat in a huge old chair, a dilapidated recliner with a table at the side covered with cracker crumbs and cough drops. A bowl of butterscotch candies was mostly empty, and the yellow wrappers that once held them were distributed across his lap, over his arms, and across the table. Beyond the table they spilled onto the floor and piled up into an uneven mound.

The fireplace had little blowers on each side, and the air they moved blew the occasional falling wrapper across the carpeted floor onto the linoleum of the kitchen and, once there, onward to parts unknown.

The drone of the fans and the low growl of the TV aggravated Grant's fragile brain and caused him to grit his teeth.

Standing Bear was holding a coffee cup, but Sam knew it wasn't coffee. Without saying anything, he gently removed the cup from Bear's grasp, carried it into the kitchen, and poured it into the sink.

"That's good whiskey," Bear said.

"I thought you were asleep."

"That was pretty good stuff."

"I brought you a surprise."

Bear's eyes brightened, and he turned to look at Grant. "Sam," he said. "I thought you were Nathan or one of the women."

"Straight from France. I ordered it last week."

"Chablis?"

"Your favorite."

"Get yourself a cup, too."

Grant collected the pieces of yellow cellophane off the kitchen floor and in the living room under the table and chair. He could look down now without sickening but not without pain behind his eyes. He cleaned Bear's lap and arms and brushed the crumbs and filth from the table into a kitchen trash can.

"You look like crap," the Bear said. "What's wrong with your face?"

"It's called Bell's palsy."

"Is it catching?"

"No, sir. It's harmless."

"Because there is this stuff out there that is catching."

"I know, Father."

"I've been sitting here all winter. Did you catch the stuff?"

"No. I was vaccinated."

"They poked you with a needle?"

"Twice."

"Good God."

Grant wiped down the kitchen counters, found a clean cup, and poured the wine. "When do the women clean?"

"What day is this?"

"It is Sunday."

He shrugged. "I don't know. Not Sunday. Nobody cares anymore. Nobody hardly comes. I used to run things."

"You still run things."

"Damn right. I still run things. Where have you been? It's a year since I've seen you."

"I was injured. Then the pandemic came, and I thought it was best not to visit."

"What have you been doing? More witchcraft?"

"I've been studying with Mr. Brebeuf. I think you know him."

"I know him. He's a witch, too. Like your grandmother, the old hag."

"You loved my grandmother."

"Did I say otherwise?"

"I think Grandma is angry at you."

"I know she is."

"Does she come to you too, in your dreams?"

"She comes."

"I haven't felt her presence in a long time, but I started again today, coming here."

"It's the plane crash. She blames me."

"It was an accident. It doesn't seem to me you did anything so wrong."

"People died."

Grant sighed. "Yes, they did."

"I wanted to protect my people. Instead, I endangered them. What do you do with Brebeuf?"

"We do the old stories."

"Which ones?"

"Aayaash. Wenebojo."

"Kids' stuff."

"Right now, I am studying the story of Sky Woman."

Standing Bear belched loudly. "It's crap," he said.

"She left her children here on earth," Grant continued. "On this unstable planet." The old patriarch belched again. "I'm trying to figure out what Sky Woman knew."

"Jack squat," he said. "She knew jack squat."

"No, Father. I am serious. That is what I am trying to do."

"This is how your fill your days?"

"Not entirely. Mostly, I guess.

"What has happened to you? You were a big man. You have shrunk into the body of an old woman."

"The spirits punish me."

"Bull crap."

"I was injured in Paraguay. I am still... recovering."

"Recovering, my eye. Do you suppose there is anything that happens to you that I don't know about? The gossip arrives days ahead of you, when you come at all."

"Does it bring wine?"

He smiled. "It's excellent. Like in the war when I was over there. Come sit down. Why haven't you come?"

"I told you. I thought it best. I am old and you are, what, 90?"

Standing Bear waved it away with his hand. "What is age?"

"To a virus, we both look like roadkill."

"They want to stick me with that needle."

"The women from the clinic?"

"Yes."

"You should do that."

He made a fart sound with his mouth. "What do they know? They stuck you, and look what happened."

"It wasn't the vaccination."

"It was the hanging. Do you suppose I don't know these things? They kidnapped you in that far country and they hung you. You should not have gone to that place. Now look at you."

"I am being punished."

"You punish yourself."

"Father, you seem to know everything. Do you you know why I am here?"

"It is not to get my blessing."

"No."

"It is not because you are a good son."

"No, Father. I am not."

"It is because of that plane crash."

"I need that case. That metal case."

"I know nothing about any metal case. How's that? Whatever you suspect me of, I am innocent."

"Putting those snow machines across the bay looks like your work. Nathan would have done it better."

"Oh, would he now? How can you be sure? Do you think he's ready to take over this clan? To shuffle me aside?"

"What do you think?"

"I asked you the question."

"Yes," Grant said firmly. "I do. It's time, Father."

The old man softened suddenly and sighed as he settled deeper into his chair. "Maybe you are right. You are the only one who would tell me that."

"I'm sorry to be so blunt."

"No, it is good. That is the Sam Grant I knew. Maybe a piece of him lives."

"Maybe. We'll see."

"There was nothing in the case. Just papers."

"That's what I thought."

"The bucks were all excited. They thought there would be drugs or money. Diamonds, gold, jewels. What have you. Just a bunch of papers, that's all. It was a waste of time." He sighed again. "Two people died."

"Yes."

"Sooner or later they will come for us here," Standing Bear announced. "They will figure it all out and will come."

"I think the new tribal patrolman, Jacob Dewberry, had it figured all along. But he never gave you away."

"Then he is better than most of those cops."

"He would never give you away, though he had never met any of you."

"Well, that makes him the best of the bunch. We've been watching him at the bay. Sidney saved his life."

"Yes, Dewberry is grateful. He is meeting with Sidney outside right now. I should have him say hello to you."

"I am drinking wine."

"I think you have been drinking all day."

"Yes, but not Chablis. I don't know where you find it."

"I order it just for you. Father, where is the case?"

"Ask your grandmother. I'm sure she could lead you right to it, the old hag."

"I am sure she could. But it would be better if you had it brought to me. I don't want any poison between us."

"Maybe I want to keep the case."

"If you keep it, the FBI will come for it. And the people it belongs to will want it back. They are violent men, and very dangerous."

Standing Bear used his unsteady right hand to wave away that notion. "We are safe here."

"It's just *joganosh* stuff. Why not give it back to them?"

"Why do you ask this of me? Because you work for them?"

"I don't work for anyone. Look at me. Who would hire me?" Grant pulled his chair up close and put his face near Standing Bear. He puts his hands on the old man's massive arms, grown soft with disuse. "Father, have someone bring me the case, and then let me call the clinic when I get home and have them bring you out the vaccine. Then you can enjoy the closeness of people again. See their smiles. Feel their touch. I ask these things because they are in your best interest, and for no other reason."

"You talk like those doctors in those soap shows in the afternoon."

"And you are not convinced."

"I am old. I don't know who to trust. You are a witch, and those others, on those shows, are as bad or worse."

Grant shrugged. "You will do the right thing in the end. You always do."

"I don't even think they are real doctors."

"No. They are actors."

"I think they are just there for the women."

Grant pushed aside a curtain and watched Dewberry talking happily with the young man who had saved his life. Bearbait and a couple of children were building a snow Indian, complete with a feather on top.

"You are still a great man, Father," he said softly. Bear just grunted. "And what you do is valuable. The *joganosh* out there have no clans. They have no neighbors whose duty it is to look out for them. They just have cops and nurses they have to hire and pay."

"Even here, the old ways are passing."

"Yes."

"Young people don't know the stories, the traditions."

"There are good ones." Dewberry had pulled up his sleeve and was showing his wrist and arm to the young man named Sidney. "Let me introduce you to one."

THIRTY-FIVE

"WOW, HE'S EVEN bigger than I thought," Dewberry whistled as they climbed back onto the snowmobile. "He's like a giant. That must be where you get your size."

"You seem to have this thing about size," Grant hissed. "It doesn't mean anything."

"It does to some people."

"Well, stay away from those people."

"He shook my hand," Dewberry said reverently. "Standing Bear shook my hand. And he smiled. Is that good?"

"If you're going to work here at Red Cliff for a long time, Standing Bear is someone you will want to know. He is the best source you will find. Nathan, too. I think he will take over soon."

"Nathan seems a little stand-offish. Maybe he doesn't trust cops."

"What about the guy named Sidney?"

"He's really cool. Just a kid. But I think we could be friends. What he did was really dangerous. He crawled out on that ice and put a loop around my hand. Nobody else was there. We could have both died. Are you ready to go?"

"Not quite. Let's sit here a minute."

"How come?"

"Just for a little while."

"It's cold."

"Just wait. My grandmother is telling me to wait, and when she does, I wait."

"How long?"

"Maybe twenty minutes. I don't know. Maybe an hour."

"An hour! Everyone is looking at us, wondering what we're doing."

"Yes. And Standing Bear is in his house looking at us. That's the point."

Dewberry shut off the engine. Then Bearbait shut his down, too. "Well, we'll save the gas then."

"That's good. Jacob Dewberry, there are many things I like about you. One of them is that I think you are a person who knows how to wait."

Dewberry turned his collar up and adjusted his gloves. "If this is a game, I can play it as well as anyone."

The time passed and Dewberry talked about his rescue. "Did you see Sidney's dog?"

"I saw," Grant affirmed.

"He's a Newfoundland, a 'newfie,' Sidney calls him. His name is Ben. He's 180 pounds, jet black and shaggy as a bear. Shaggier maybe."

"Even his head looks like a bear. To a drowning man, it would be an easy mistake."

"Did you know newfies are bred for water rescue? It's in their genes. He rushed right up to me in the ice. Sidney got the belt around my wrist and gave the other end to Ben. He took it in his teeth and just kept backing up. He pulled me right out of the ice and all the way to shore. His feet are huge and they're actually webbed, like an otter. He must have the power of a small bulldozer, but he's just as friendly and sweet as a puppy."

"It was all very lucky."

"It's a lesson to me as a you know, police officer. Don't jump to conclusions. Don't go thinking something supernatural happened when there may be a perfectly natural explanation."

"It's a good lesson."

"Yeah, but it doesn't explain you and your dead grandmother and the guard's snowmobile."

"Jacob, I always think there's a natural explanation. We just don't know everything about the natural world."

They had been there about forty-five minutes, and everyone outside had gone in, one at a time. The three men on the two snowcats were alone listening to the wind howl when they heard a door slam on a distant house. Before long, a woman came into sight. She was wearing furs and knee-high moccasins and carrying a bag. She was not wearing snowshoes, so it took her a long time to reach the men on the snowmobiles. She said nothing, just reached into the bag and pulled out a silver case about the size of two briefcases. She handed it to Grant, who said thank you. Then she turned and left.

"Holy crap. Is that what I think it is?" Jacob asked.

"It's just papers."

"Is that what we've been waiting for?"

"No. We were waiting for Standing Bear to make up his mind. And since we were freezing, we were putting a little pressure on him." Grant smiled. "The old guy always comes through in the end."

"Are you going to take that to Agent Tuba?"

"Nope. I'm going to take it to Sheriff Inconsequential. Let him give it to Tuba."

"Sheriff who?"

"Radisson. The guy the feds all ignore."

"Sweet."

Dewberry started the snowmobile and the two men began the trek back up the old lane. Near the end they reached the guard with the faulty snowcat. He was stomping around and beating his hands on his chest, trying to keep feeling in them.

"What did Nathan say about me?" the guard wanted to know.

"He said you were a good man."

"That's bull. Is someone going to come get me?"

"I think your snowcat will start now. Try it."

"I already did. About a hundred times. It's dead. It won't start."

"Try it again."

The buck muttered something under his breath, adjusted the choke and pulled the rope. The snowcat roared to life.

"Get yourself home to a nice warm fire," Grant said. "I'm sorry for your discomfort."

THIRTY-SIX

W HEN THEY got back to Grant's truck, Dewberry and Bodette drove the snowmobiles onto the trailer and shut them off.

"So now I've met your father," Jacob said. "And, I think, your grandmother too."

"Yeah, she's a hoot, isn't she?"

They dropped off Bodette at his mother's home and drove back to the deserted station. Then Grant turned to talk to Dewberry.

"Are you going to open the case?" Dewberry wondered.

"No. I don't care what's inside. Do you?"

"Nope."

"I'm just going to take it to the sheriff right now."

"That's good. The sooner it's over, the better."

"Standing Bear said it was just papers. What could they be worth?"

"They're worth $500,000," Dewberry said without hesitation.

"I thought you would say that."

"It's useless to lie to you. You've figured it all out, I'm sure. I've never met anyone quite like you."

"It was stupid to send those emails."

"It was not. I had to stop those people from digging around on the reservation. They would have hurt someone."

"Perhaps. Yes."

"Once they thought somebody had already found the case and taken it off the reservation, we were safe."

"But sooner or later they would find out it was a hoax."

"I figured by then the FBI would have the case and it would be all wrapped up."

"You might have been wrong," Grant suggested.

"I wasn't."

"Whatever you do in this world has consequences beyond your ability to see. When suspicion falls on you, it falls on me and on those around you."

"I'm sorry if that happened."

"Jacob, you are a young man. You are comfortable with risk, as I once was. But you were messing with awfully powerful and dangerous men."

"Worse than the Taliban? Than ISIS?"

"No. I understand your spirit. You are brave and strong and very confident. You have already, at your young age, seen and done many hard things in far-off places. Just be careful. You don't want to end up like me."

Dewberry looked at Grant for a long time. "That wouldn't be so bad," he said softly.

"Do you know the story of Aayaash and the bad man in the *mudookwan*?"

"Yes, Aayaash was traveling with a wise old fox, his protector. I guess the fox is you. The bad man tried to poison Aayaash, but the fox warned Aayaash and saved him by eating the poison himself. So-o-o-o, I guess you've warned me. Right?"

"Yes."

"And it all ends well. I'm saved and the bad men don't hurt me."

"I suppose," Grant said. "But let's not forget the fox had to eat the poison."

Dewberry laughed. "Story understood," he said. "Thank you."

THIRTY-SEVEN

SAM GRANT was pretty sure this was not a good idea. Though it was a beautiful day, clear and blue and sunny, the road he was driving was not maintained in the winter, and the nearest human outpost was well behind and receding. But Harold Brebeuf was all smiles.

"It's three or four more miles to the lakeshore," Grant said. "And I don't think my phone will work out here. If we get stuck, neither of us can walk out."

"Then don't get stuck," Brebeuf said, the smile never fading.

"I don't know Bad River as well as I do Red Cliff. Aren't we headed toward where they had the Feast of the Dead?"

"We are a little west of there. We are going to a place called Honest John Lake. Do you know it?"

"No."

"It is a little lake right next to the big lake," Brebeuf explained. "There is just a strip of sand that separates them. Just a beach and a trail. I am told the big lake is rising and will soon swallow the little lake. It is a place important to your people. A holy place. I have to see it one more time."

"Everything will be frozen, Uncle. Both lakes. And covered with snow."

"We will find it. Others will be there. It is a sacred day."

"I don't know anything special about today. It is not a feast day." But the road to the Lake Superior shore was in fact deeply rutted with fresh truck tracks. So Grant followed them obediently.

When they reached the shoreline, they turned west and followed the narrow road to where it ended in a loop. But the tracks left the road, crossed over a dune and onto the edge of the beach, now almost bare because the wind blew so hard here that the snow was swept away.

Grant stopped, but Brebeuf urged him on. "It's okay," he said. "It's all frozen. The sand and the water. It is the only time of the year you can drive to Honest John Lake. It is not far now."

The northeast wind swept down from Isle Royal and all the way across the great lake. A gust slammed into the side of Grant's pickup so hard it literally banged on the metal. So did the next gust. Soon the banging was so loud the two old men could not speak.

Grant thought about the moose and the wolves on Isle Royal, a closed community of predators and prey, undisturbed by the outside world, coexisting there for generations. What can one say about such a place? That it is good, because nature is in balance? Or it is bad, because everyone lives amid murder and loss?

What would Sky Woman say?

It was obvious when they reached Honest John because the lake was bare ice, with pellets of frozen snow whipping across it. Grant would have stopped, except that he could see a couple of vehicles parked a long way ahead, and there was no way here to turn around.

The vehicles were parked on the beach. Above them, on a raised strip of land between Honest John and Lake Superior, a ceremonial *wiigiwaam* had been pitched. It was made of buckskin stretched over sturdy aspen poles and then covered with birch bark.

Brebeuf led Grant through the low opening into the smoky interior. A big fire burned in the middle, and instantly Grant understood why he was here.

Seated cross-legged near the fire was Jennifer Deedeens, who said nothing to him and stared straight ahead. A very old woman he had once met, named Two Teeth, was also there, propped against a large bag that created a backrest. Brebeuf introduced Grant to three other men already seated around the fire. Grant had never seen them before, and Brebeuf had used only their Anishinaabe names.

Each person sitting in the circle had *miigis* shells laid out in front of them. Deedeens had just one. Brebeuf had four. Two Teeth had three. The other men each had two. Around the fire there were two empty spaces, each of which had three shells.

"You are to sit here, Crow Eyes." The old man seemed in an especially good mood. "As you can see, we are missing two members who are unable to be here today. But we have placed *miigis* shells in the place they would sit. Do you know about these shells?"

"In the Land of the Dawn," Grant began, "seven *miigis* rose from the sea and gave the Ojibwe a prophecy. They said that many people would be coming from across the sea, and would kill those who remained in the Land."

"And what is the Land of the Dawn?"

"The Eastern Place, the east coast of America. It is where the Ojibwe are from."

"And what did the Ojibwe do?"

"The *miigis* told the people to move west, along the string of great lakes, to avoid the invaders. That's what we did, long before the white people arrived. As a result we had less trouble, and we were able to keep many of our homelands. Or at least pieces of them."

Brebeur seemed anxious to have Grant continue. "What else do you know about this shell?"

"It is the symbol of the Midewiwin Society. A secret society of healers and seers."

"And can you keep this secret?"

"Yes, but I have not asked to come here today. It is not clear why I am here."

"Crow Eyes, this society is not something you apply for. Those of us here do not choose the members. Such choices are made by the ancients and exhibited in special ways, through healing and seeing.

"When it is clear that some person among us lives close to the spirit world and has learned the cures, the songs and the stories, we gather on a special day and quiz that person to make sure his knowledge is adequate and his powers are proven.

"Your powers are well known to all of us, Crow Eyes. I, and your grandmother before me, have taught you what we can. Today we will find out if it is adequate."

"The final exam?" Grant asked.

The old woman leaned forward and looked Grant straight in the eyes. "We have all been through many trials, Crow Eyes. And our bodies, like yours, show the wear. The ancients are not gentle with us. They live in a spirit world and cannot do things with their hands and feet. Instead, they ask us to do those things. What they ask is often difficult. Sometimes impossible."

She leaned back against the bag and closed her eyes. "You will be tested today, yes. But it is nothing compared to the tests already behind you, or the tests that lie ahead."

With that, Deedeens began asking Grant about roots and barks and berries, about diseases and formulations for cures. She had known Grant for a long time and did not believe his knowledge was complete. She had studied under Grant's grandmother for many years. While a brilliant woman, a physicist by training, Deedeens had struggled to learn it all. She could not believe that Grant just suddenly remembered perfectly everything his grandmother had taught him as a boy.

Grant answered every question confidently and without hesitation.

One of the men leaned forward and asked, "What is your relationship right now with the spirit of your grandmother?"

"I don't know," Grant said. "I never know. She comes and goes. I'm never sure it is even her."

"When I was a boy, I visited your grandmother because I had a rash that would not go away. She gave me a paste to put on that rash. She put it in an odd container because she was poor and couldn't find anything else. Can you tell me what she put it in?"

Grant closed his eyes, sighed, and just waited a minute in the silence around the fire. It was warm in the *wiigiwaam* and suddenly very comfortable. The wind seemed far away.

"She cut off the toe of an old nylon sock she was wearing and put the paste in that. Then she took you outside and showed you the bush that was causing the rash. She ran her hands over the bush and told you it was not poison. She said the bush was sorry for the pain it caused you, but it was not the bush's fault. It was your own body reacting to the bush in an unfriendly way. She told you to make friends with the bush, and you would be untroubled by it for the rest of your life."

The man grinned and leaned back. "And I did what she said. I made friends with the sumac. And that was the start of my journey here."

Finally, Brebeuf intervened.

"Some of us are old and can't sit like this very long. Before we leave, I want you to tell us the story of Aayaash and the flaming arrows. Tell it the very best way you can."

Grant thought for a moment.

"We know the Aayaash stories are very old because of the descriptions of shelters and dwelling places and tools. The story goes like this:

"When Aayaash was a young man, he was falsely accused of mating with his father's youngest wife. The father took Aayaash far out into the lake, to a barren island, to get bird eggs. When Aayaash left the canoe, the father paddled off and left his son for dead.

"But Aayaash had a helping spirit, his grandmother, and the next day a horned serpent swam by and offered Aayaash a ride to shore. His troubles continued through many adventures and close encounters with death, until he found his way back to his village.

"There he had a terrible dream that the world was about to be destroyed by fire. It was a vivid dream, and he was convinced it was true.

"His father kept a large bag of fat and food and other necessities for use in an emergency. Aayaash told his father about the dream and begged for that bag. He told his father that if they had a ceremony and sacrificed this bag of reserves, they might all be saved. But his father would not believe the dream and would not make the sacrifice.

"So Aayaash went into the woods and cleared a small area. In it he drew a circle in the earth. In the circle he put a bow and four magic arrows.

"He returned to the village and implored his mother to come with him into the woods. He had her stand with him inside the circle, where he said they would both be safe.

"Then he fired a flaming arrow into the east, and the Earth erupted in fire. Not just the land, but the waters as well, so that nearly everything was killed."

"His father ran screaming into the woods and begged to join them in the circle. But Aayaash refused. He told his father to take his young wife and crawl into the bag of reserves, and there they might find safety. But soon the bag caught fire and they were killed.

"When all was destroyed, Aayaash turned to his mother and said, "We cannot live anymore as humans. The land will not support us. So he turned her into a robin, and himself into a toad.

"Eventually the Earth grew back, greener than before, and it blossomed with new life."

When Grant was done, everyone nodded.

"What is the significance of the bag?" Brebeuf asked.

"There are people who always prepare for end times," Grant said. "It will not save them."

"Why was the arrow fired into the east?"

"It has always been the direction from which bad things come."

"Why did Aayaash turn his mother into a robin?"

"Because he knew the world would need something beautiful in it, something with a song, to bring light in the morning."

"And why did Aayaash turn himself into a toad? Did the world also need something ugly?"

"I used to think that. I don't anymore."

"Why then?"

"Because it is what he deserved."

There was a long silence, which Brebeuf finally broke.

"Tell me this, Crow Eyes. Aayaash and his flaming arrow— is that just an old Ojibwe story?"

"No," Grant said firmly. "It is a prophecy."

THIRTY-EIGHT

FOR A LONG time, nobody in the *wiigiwaam* said anything. Finally, they all stood except Grant and Brebeuf, his teacher. They circled the fire, passing around behind the two seated men. Grant kept his face forward, and occasionally someone passing behind would snap Grant's head with his or her finger. Sometimes someone would put something on his head, kind of weaving it into his hair.

When they had all left the tent, and Brebeuf could hear their trucks outside starting, he put his hand on Grant's shoulder and used it to raise himself.

"Hard on this old body," he moaned.

Grant ran his fingers through his hair and started pulling out *miigis*.

"How many?" Brebeuf asked.

"Three," Grant said.

The old man nodded.

"Do you understand what is required of you now?"

"Yes."

"You must be a teacher, like your grandmother."

"I understand."

"You will need to find a student."

"I found one. But he is not Bear Clan."

Brebeuf shrugged. "Then make it work."

"I never in my life dreamed I would become a Midew."

"It is not something you become. It is something you are. You have been a Midew for many years, probably since you were a child. Your grandmother knew it. I knew it. We just wanted you to be a good one." Brebeuf looked down on Grant's face: unshaved, one eye closed, stringy hair. "Well," he said, "I can hope for the best."

Brebeuf stepped up close behind Grant and put his hands on his shoulders. "You have suffered enough," he said.

"Yes."

"Your grandmother is here. Can you feel her?"

"Yes."

"And the others?"

"I can hear their feet. Moccasins in the sand. They are dancing. There are drums."

"They are very near. They were always here."

"Yes."

"They could have healed you whenever you wanted."

"I wasn't ready."

"Are you ready now?"

"I want to know what Sky Woman knew when she left her children on this planet."

"You already know."

"I don't, my uncle. I have tried so hard."

"You were told."

"I wasn't. I … I thought … " Grant dropped his head. "Yes," he said. "I was told."

"And do you now understand?"

"Yes, Uncle."

And then it started falling, the fine ash, the tiny, warm crystals of nothing. They fell all around Grant, tumbling down his head and arms. He looked up so they would fall on his distorted face. He stretched his legs out and caught as many as he could. He sat like that, with his eyes closed, while the sound of the drums and dancing faded away, far into the distance, and then disappeared.

"It never gets old, seeing this," Brebeuf said.

"No. It's wonderful."

"It's time to go. We need to get out of here before dark."

Grant jumped to his feet and stood straight and tall.

"I think you just grew five inches," Brebeuf said. "I had forgotten how big you are. How is your leg?"

"Perfect," Grant said. "He opened and closed the bad hand. Everything is perfect."

"Can you remember the hanging now?"

"No. My memory is the same."

"If your body doesn't want you to remember it, then you shouldn't remember it. Your eye is open."

"I can see. The double vision is gone."

"Excellent," said the old man. "Now please find another place to sleep. The missus is tired of you."

"I bet."

"Go back to your other house, the one in Bayfield. And don't burn it down."

THIRTY-NINE

GRANT UNLOCKED the gate and pulled into the courtyard behind the big Victorian house. The woman who owned it was never there in the winter. For that matter, she wasn't there much in the summer. Grant did not know her story. But he was happy to rent her garage with the guest house above. It was cheap and had good light and no mice.

It was home. Bayfield was home, the little town on the big hill that arched around the great lake. It didn't have a Walmart or even a Goodwill. Main Street was two blocks long. But it had a bookstore, a coffee shop, and a couple of good restaurants. It also had a grocery store of sorts, but it was old and small, with an uneven wood plank floor.

Bayfield had a fine marina and a great pier you could tie up to and walk around town, as well as the landing for ferry boats to Madeline Island.

And it had a thousand wonderful smells and sounds and memories. He had spent every summer with his grandmother at nearby Red Cliff, and had spent every nickel he could find in Bayfield shops.

Yes, it was home, and he had never been so happy to be there. He unlocked the garage and opened the big door. His sailboat was dusty, unused for two years. He ran his hand along the fiberglass gunnel as he walked its length. He gave the winch a spin and smiled when it clicked around smoothly. He had lived in the boat in Bayfield's marina before he found the garage to rent. So here were both his homes: the cottage on top, with the boat in its womb.

He walked to the rear of the house and checked the gauge on the propane tank. Enough for now, until he could get a truck out.

The stairs that went up the outside of the garage were snowbound. Since Paraguay, they had been an insurmountable barrier to normal life. But he was well again, and he went up easily. He would shovel later. He wanted to get inside.

The cottage was one small bedroom in back, with a little bath off of it. A large living room, with two great windows, had a good hardwood floor. A kitchen was in front: long, narrow, and sunny.

He lit the gas wall furnace. It was below freezing in the house but there was a little wood in the box, so he got the wood stove going, too.

He had supposed a racket outside was something tossing about in the wind. But when it didn't stop, he opened the front door. Lewis was there, halfway up the stairs, shoveling everything clean.

"Lewis, if you don't beat everything."

"Sam! The lady across the street dialed 9-1-1 when she saw some old man messing with the gate. She got your license number, so I knew it was you."

"Is that what she said, 'some old man?'"

"I thought I'd shovel your steps. I knew it would be a struggle for you."

"I'm a lot better," Grant said.

"Are you here to stay?"

"Here to stay, Lewis. And so happy to be here again."

"I'm happy to have you back. I like having someone to share a hot Alpine with on a cold night. I've missed you."

"I've missed me, too." Grant laughed. "I wasn't sure I'd ever be back to normal."

"Let's have a look at you." Radisson reached the landing at the top of the stairs. He put the shovel down, put his hand under Grant's chin and turned his face side-to-side.

"Your eyes are wide open again."

"Look at this." Grant held up his once useless hand and opened and closed his fist. "The muscles are weak, but I can move everything just fine."

"And walk."

"No problem."

"That's wonderful, Sam. You know, I always thought that what you had could be something that would just go away someday, just as fast as it came. Brains are funny things."

"Come in, Lewis. I've got a fire going."

"I'm on duty, Sam. Look at that view." From the landing atop the stairs, they could look down on the town and the wharf, on the frozen lake and, on the horizon, Madeline Island shrouded in mist. "I always liked this place."

"You found it for me."

"Yes, I did. And I'm happy you're back."

"Did you get that case to Agent Tuba?"

"Yes, I did." Radisson smiled ear to ear. "It was about the best day of my life. You should have seen him."

"He'll probably take the credit."

"There's what's called a chain of evidence. It's a document that records everyone who has possessed a piece of important stuff. At the top is "Confidential Informant." The next name on it is mine. Then Tuba goes on third. That's third, Sam, right behind me and you. Man, that must grate on him."

"Did you open it?"

"Nope. It was locked, just like you found it. Whatever is in it, it's federal business. But Sam, thanks for everything you did. I couldn't have done any of it, not on that reservation. Tomorrow is Saturday. Why don't you come over in the afternoon? Jackie will make meatloaf and we can play cards afterward."

"Sounds wonderful. How about Sunday? I've got kind of big day planned tomorrow."

"Sunday it is." Radisson carried the shovel down the stairs and put it in the still-open garage. Grant followed. He took his hat off and wiped his brow with his sleeve. "Man. It's been some winter."

Grant put his arms around Radisson and held him tight. "My old friend," he said. "Thank you so much."

"I only shoveled your steps," Lewis said.

"For everything," Grant said. "Thanks for everything. You've been a wonderful friend."

FORTY

SATURDAY MORNING, Grant stopped at the grocery store and picked up a small roast, potatoes, an onion, and a great big carrot.

The long drive into Charlie Weegwasi's place had been unused for a week. Grant put the truck in four-wheel drive, but it staggered and slipped and he quickly gave it up. Instead, he backed onto the plowed highway and put chains on the rear wheels. It took half an hour of heavy effort, and he was glad for the work after so much idle time.

With chains the truck made it fine, the front bumper and grill plowing snow as it went. He got as close as he could to the front porch and walked through a crotch-high drift to the front door. It was still wrapped with police tape. Grant pulled it all down, then wadded it up and stuck it in the pocket of his down coat.

He pushed the door open and went inside. Nothing had been touched. It was just like it was the moment Weegwasi left it, running out into the blizzard. There was kindling in a big basket next to the cast-iron cookstove. Grant found matches and started a fire, piling on bigger pieces of wood as it flared.

It was an inside fire, Grant decided—a fire contained within a vessel, harnessed for useful service to mankind. His house fire had been an outside fire. It had become itself a vessel, holding in its womb the pictures and memorabilia, the last remnants of his early life. It had consumed it all, and provided no useful service.

The forest fires then burning in California were a different level still. They were fires that had turned on the humans with vicious intent, moving rapidly across the land, destroying everything they could reach and belching clouds of soot and smoke to places far away.

What must the fire be like that is lit by Aayaash's arrow?

Fires do not think, but neither do viruses. Yet both have a purpose, and it is malignant. We can use the world to our benefit for a while, if we are careful with it. But we are fragile little sticks of carbon on an unstable planet. When we believe we are anything more than that, the planet can bring us down with nothing more than a shrug of its shoulders.

The cabin was warming, so Grant cut the roast into stew-sized pieces and dried them and rolled them in flour. When the skillet on the front of the stove was hot, the meat was browned in oil and then transferred to a big cast-iron pot, full of boiling water, with the potatoes and pieces of carrot. He added salt and pepper, parsley, and a package of dried onion soup mix. A little flour would give it body.

He put a lid on the pot and moved it to the back of the stove to simmer.

Grant pulled his parka tight around him and trudged back to the truck to put on his snowshoes. He would find Charlie Weegwasi today. And then he would celebrate. He would not wait until spring, after the critters emerged from their holes, hungry for rancid meat.

He looked around for wolves or a *wiindigoog*, and seeing none, headed to the edge of the clearing. There were three trails through the brush, radiating outward like spokes of a wheel. He had taken the middle one last time and had found the blood. This time he would take the one to the right.

The trail wound through a dense forest of white pine and aspen, but eventually came out onto mostly open country. Underneath was Canadian shield, massive blocks of rock long ago scoured by glaciers during one of Earth's little tantrums. Between the great blocks were little ribbons of earth, and on them many raspberry bushes, and ivy and fern and small trees had found root.

With everything covered by snow, the rivulets of flora ran like veins across the landscape, and Grant followed them. He kept his mind clear, trying not to think, trying to be open to inspiration.

Sam Grant was in the space between science and faith, and he had found the balance. He looked out across the land to see what he could see. But he could not see the electromagnetic waves streaming from pole to pole. He could not see the tiny vibrations from water and objects underground that could be found by any good witcher. There were unseen particles of solar radiation streaming all around. There were electrons breaking free from their nuclei and running wildly away. The unseen things outnumbered the seen things by a million to one, and Grant listened to the voices of the unseen things.

On one of the brushy seams there was a mound rising out of the snow. Not a high mound, but something nature would not have shaped by itself. Grant looked at the mound from fifty yards away and knew it was Charlie Weegwasi. He walked up slowly and examined the little stumps in the bushes until he could see that one of them was an iron pipe, rusted and nearly invisible.

Grant put his mouth to the pipe and said softly, "Charlie, are you down there?" He listened for a while but heard nothing. So he asked again, louder this time.

Finally, a distant voice, a high-pitched, feeble voice, came up through the pipe. "Who … who is dat?"

FORTY-ONE

SAM GRANT lowered his head and closed his eyes and took a deep breath. "Charlie, it's Sam Grant. Do you remember me? I came to take you home."

"Are you a *wiindigoog?*"

"No, Charlie. I am a friend. Can I come down?"

"Dare are many *bagwajiwinii* up dare. Day can get in your nose."

"I know. I've been vaccinated. I have no *bagwajiwinii.*"

"Wid a needle, like da fat woman brings?"

"Yes."

"Did it hurt?"

"Only a little. Can I come down?"

"Da snow has covered da door. I can't push it open."

"Knock on it and I will find it."

It was like a cellar door, almost horizontal, made from uneven old boards hanging on rusty hinges. Grant used a snowshoe to dig down to it and then, on his hands and knees, he used his mittened hand to brush it clean.

The door opened with a belch of musty, earthen air. Two small, watery eyes looked up at him and then scrambled away into the recesses of the hole. "You are da one dat put me in jail."

"No. Charlie. I talked to you there, but I didn't put you there. I didn't want you there. Really."

Grant crawled into the hole and discovered it was more like a cavern. The ground had been excavated to below the great rocks on either side, and then under the rocks, so that the space was mostly walled and roofed by solid granite. He could easily stand but could hardly see. The only light was a candle at the far end, maybe twenty feet away, the light that came down the ventilation pipe, and now the overcast light that came through the open door.

When his eyes adjusted, he could see green and red veins running through the rock walls. He walked over and touched one. It was a seam of pure copper and copper ore.

Protruding from the soil beneath the rocks were the handles of buried baskets. Dozens of them. No, more like hundreds. Grant caught his breath. "This is where you season your baskets."

"Da soil here makes dem pretty," he said. "How did you find me?"

"My grandmother helped," Grant said. He sat down cross-legged on the soft earth floor and placed in front of him the three *miigis* shells. "I was given these shells this week in a birch-covered *wiigiwaam* at a ceremonial place on the lake."

Charlie, who had been cowering against the back wall, took a step closer to see. Grant kept talking softly.

"In the circle around the fire, there were two empty spaces." Charlie picked up the candle and took another step, and then another. "I think one of them was yours."

Charlie sat down cross-legged opposite Grant and put the candle between them. He opened his shirt and took off the medicine bag hanging around his neck. From it he extracted three *miigis* and put them on the ground in front him. "I am sorry," he said. "I could not attend." He held his palms out in a gesture that said, "You can see why."

"The other empty space, I think, belongs to Standing Bear, my father."

"We are getting old," Charlie said. "And maybe lazy too. Udders do da healing now."

"That is why the Bear Clan never came looking for you. Standing Bear knew you were safe."

"I am almost out of food. I don't dink I could have waited for spring to clear my door."

"You have water?"

"Yes. Do you want some? It comes from a little spring."

"What do you use for a bathroom?"

"I have a hole over dare," he said. "I cover it wid a little dirt each time. It is getting full."

"It's time to go home, Charlie."

Weegwasi looked around with sadness in his eyes. "I suppose," he said. "I like it here. It is safe."

"And you make baskets there," Grant said, pointing to a yard-wide circle of light that came down through the pipe, and the pile of lashing and reeds and willow and bark that surrounded it.

"When da light is right."

"It is good to go home."

"It is all home," he said. "When our people came into dis land, da great ice sheet was still here. Da great lake had not been made. We are older dan da land."

"The ice left you these great rocks and this perfect sanctuary."

"I don't dink our home wants us here anymore," he said softly. "I dink it will send us away now. We made too many mistakes. I am braiding horsehair for da rim of dis basket. It will go all da way around, so I will be braiding for a long time. And when I am done, I will tie off da strands in tiny little knots, so small you can hardly see dem. But if I miss just one knot, just one tiny knot, it will all unravel.

"When I look back, I see da time we stopped hunting and starting planting. It was no good for us, because it made da land more valuable dan da animals. It made owners and servants. Den we started building cities, and dis was not good either, because cities filled up wid people who make no food. But I dink we were still okay den. We were still partners wid da animals. Day pulled da plows and da barges up da canals. Day didn't need gasoline. Da bad day was da day we created da machines. Day replaced da animals. We started wrecking our home for da wood and da coal and da metals to feed da machines. From dat day, I dink, da braid unraveled. I dink we missed a knot."

"We missed many knots, Charlie. Many, many knots," Grant observed.

"Da white people, day dink day can fix dis braid. Day dink day can do anything. But day cannot fix dis."

"Charlie, I don't think they've figured out what Sky Woman knew. Let's go home."

FORTY-TWO

GRANT HELD Weegwasi's arm and helped him along the trail. Grant had snowshoes but Charlie had woven basket strips stretched over a willow frame. And, of course, knee-high moccasins.

"Why did you run away, Charlie? Were you afraid of a *wiindigoog?*"

"He looked in my window. He had big yellow eyes and big feet."

"I think the big eyes were just a mask, Charlie. And the feet were snowshoes made to look like bird feet."

"Where would a *wiindigoog* get such a mask?"

"He could make it, if he wanted to scare an old basket maker."

"He must be very bad."

"Maybe not so bad, Charlie. Do you know who this *wiindigoog* was?"

"Yes. I dink so," Weegwasi said, but he kept his head down and didn't say anything else.

"I think it was your grandson."

"It was. When I left da house, I could hear him screaming. He was fighting wid da wolves."

"They tore him up real bad, Charlie. They broke a bone. When I saw him, he was in a cast and lots of big bandages."

"Da wolves don't like *wiindigoog*. Me eider."

"Your grandson had fallen from *ninoododadiwin*. His business was failing and his family had gone away. He was desperate for money. The man who owns the big house above you, near the lake, offered your grandson a lot of money for a paper that would allow a road to be built across your land. Your grandson faked your signature so he could have this money."

"Will my grandson go to jail?"

"Not if we don't tell anyone."

"I love my grandson."

"I know. He loves you very much. He just wanted to scare you enough so you would move into the big home in Hayward. If you moved, you would never see the road being built."

"Dis is my home."

"I understand. When your grandson found out you were missing, and probably dead, he was terribly sad. I have never seen anyone so sad. Or maybe I saw it once before. I don't want to see it again."

"I am sorry," Charlie said. "I did not know."

"It's been more than a week. Don't you think he has suffered enough?"

Charlie nodded. "Would you call him for me? Tell him to come see me."

"I called him this morning. He will come tomorrow. You must forgive him and help him find harmony again."

A hole had opened in the thinning clouds as the two old men reached the edge of the clearing. In the middle was the cabin, lit by a spotlight of sun. The light reflected by the windows danced on the snow in front. Smoke curled from the chimney.

Charlie stopped and rested and looked, but he didn't say anything.

"I have a beef stew on the stove, Charlie. I thought you would be hungry."

The old basket maker took a deep breath, held it, then let it out. A tear came down from a narrow, wet eye. "It's good to be home," he said.

FORTY-THREE

THE FOURTH of July festivities were in full swing. The lake was blue and bright and glistening in the sun. The snow had all gone away and left behind a world of deep green. That's when Jackie Radisson got the call from Jeannie Grant.

"Jeannie! What's it been? Years," Jackie squealed.

"I was hoping you would remember me," Jeannie said.

"Of course I remember you. How's Sam? I heard you two were meeting last weekend in Galena."

"That's why I called, actually."

"Did you have a good time?"

"We had an excellent time. Much better than I expected. Or hoped. Sam was great, like his old self. And he looked good. I was surprised, after the way he looked a year ago."

"That's great, Jeannie."

"But listen, I got to thinking about some of the things he said. I was thinking that maybe he and I could meet every year like that, at some of our old favorite places. But he didn't seem to want to make any plans for the future. And when he left, he gave me a very sweet kiss and said that was in case he never saw me again. I didn't think much of it at first, because he likes to kid around. But then I got worried. Jackie, I've been calling him every day for the last three or four days. He never answers. Have you or Lewis spoken to him?"

"No. I wasn't sure he was even back."

"Do you suppose that you or Lewis might stop by his place and check on him? It's probably nothing, but I'd like to know."

Sam's truck was at his Bayfield house, and the first thing Radisson noticed was a note on the steering wheel. The door was unlocked, so Lewis slid in and looked at the note.

"For Jacob Dewberry," the note said.

"Oh, my God," Jackie yelled, and went running up the stairs. "Sam?" she shouted. "Sam, it's Jackie. Are you here?"

Radisson followed her up but by the time he reached the stop of the stairs, she had barged through the unlocked door and was looking at a note attached to Grant's sofa. "For Henry Gokee," the note said. "Returned in good condition."

"Gokee bought him that sofa," Radisson said.

After that, the couple ran through the small house, reading the notes that had been attached to everything of value. The kitchen was neat and spotlessly clean. The floors had been vacuumed. A pair of shoes in the closet was newly polished. Even the little things left on the dresser and nightstand had been arranged in careful rows.

Grant's handgun and deer rifle were left to Radisson. In the closet was a box for Jackie. She put the box on the bed and opened it, then cried when she saw the brand-new bowling shoes. After that she was worthless.

"Go on home," Radisson said. "Let me try to find him. I'll start with his boat."

Jacob Dewberry was using a marina hose to wash down the cockpit of Grant's sailboat. "I've got an old girlfriend coming tomorrow," Dewberry told Radisson. "Mr. Grant told me to use the boat. He's been teaching me to sail."

"Do you know where he is?"

"Sure," Dewberry said. "He went kayaking. He said he was going to circumnavigate Lake Superior. I laughed at first, then I stopped. Mr. Grant has a way of doing what he says."

"Circumnavigate Lake Superior? That's crazy."

"Maybe."

"He's killing himself."

"He seemed pretty excited about it. Mr. Grant is someone I try not to underestimate."

"Where'd he get a kayak? Did he even do any preparation?"

"You can talk to the guy at the Adventure Shop."

"Sam Grant, ya. He bought the big one, the big sea kayak," said Swede Janssen. "I thought he bought it for a gift until he asked me to deliver it to the marina. He said he wanted to practice because it had been years."

Janssen had an open, buoyant face but a worried tone. "I told him, I said, Mr. Grant, just rent one. It's a young man's boat. You might not like it. But he wouldn't listen, you know. He bought some clothes and a bag, too. Paid cash. He said he was going to paddle around the lake and I said which lake, and he said the big lake.

"So I said, well, Mr. Grant, people don't paddle around the big lake. It's like 1,000 miles. And he says no, it's 2,000. So I said ya, and that's too far. I said why don't you sail? You have a nice big boat. And he says, no sir, he wants to get closer to the lake. He says the lake is like your lover, and you don't want to hurry with a lover.

"So I said the lake is not a lover. It is just a big tub of cold water, and it has wrecked more ships than any other water in the world. Big ships. Ocean freighters. Then I felt bad because he's boated that lake for many years and he knows it better than me I bet. So I said, it's not just the lake, Mr. Grant. It's the wind and the cold and the exhaustion. I don't think you could make that trip, and I don't think you should try."

"And he says probably not, but he said he's going to start the trip and not worry how it turns out. I said, just go out a few days and see if it's okay. I told him again to just rent a boat and he said, no sir, he couldn't promise to bring it back. That's what he said. That made me worry. But you know Sam Grant."

Radisson sighed. "Do you know when he left and which way he was going?"

"Ya. He left day before yesterday, from the marina. Paddled south toward the spit around Chequamegon. Hope he made it. That's tribal land. Maybe he will stay put there."

"He won't," Radisson said. "He'll never do what you expect. He'll go until he kills himself."

FORTY-FOUR

LEWIS RADISSON watched the otters wrestling on the end of the dock at Black River Harbor, just over the border in Michigan. A couple of adults and three juveniles were unconcerned with him or anything else. Nothing interrupted their joyful lives, lived mostly in play.

He scanned the lake with binoculars, but nothing moved. It would be dark in two hours. He would wait for that and then give it up. He couldn't think of anything else to do. Maybe call the Coast Guard. Have them keep an eye out for an old kayaker with a death wish.

The otter antics lasted another half hour before one of the adults slid smoothly into the water, and the others followed.

That opened the end of the dock for Radisson and allowed him to scan farther west. This time there was movement, low in the lake, just a few yards out from shore. Even with binoculars it was just a dark, indistinct stain against the setting sun. But there was movement on the sides of the stain, like a paddle.

"I'll be darned," he whispered. "That's 90 miles by road. Probably 65 by water, if he followed the shore. Twenty-three miles a day." He whistled.

Radisson took his shoes off and pulled his pant legs up, sat down on the dock and dangled his feet in the cold lake. After an hour he looked again with the binoculars. Sam Grant was wearing a yellow and black expedition jacket and a small yellow life preserver. He has paddling smoothly, but his face showed the strain. The kayak rolled side to side in two-foot seas. And this is a mild day, Radisson thought. Imagine six- to seven-foot seas.

Grant steered around the rock breakwater and into the small harbor. The sun was down, except for a sliver right on the horizon. The Porcupine Mountains rose up on the east side of the river, and their dark presence loomed over the harbor and picnic grounds.

"You are one hard man to find," Radisson said, his voice coming out of a shadow.

Grant jerked with mild surprise, but answered coolly, "And yet, here you are, once again."

"I wanted to see what it looked like, an old Indian committing suicide by kayak."

"Anything like you expected?"

"I want to see you get out of that thing and walk. Then I'll let you know."

Radisson pulled the kayak out onto the beach next to the boat ramp and Grant rolled onto his side, struggling out of the canvas spray skirt, groaning as he did. He couldn't get up at first, but he jammed one end of his paddle into the sand and pushed himself upright. On his feet, he staggered, but the paddle kept him from falling.

"Yeah, just about like I thought," Radisson said softly.

"Hard on the old legs," Grant admitted.

"You're going to kill yourself. I thought you already had. Jeannie called and then Jackie and I went to your place looking for you. We found all the notes."

"Did Jackie find her shoes?"

"She sure did."

Grant smiled. "I thought that was a nice touch."

"What are you doing, Sam?"

"I'm trying to fall in love again, Lewis. Fall in love with this world."

"Can't you do it somewhere safer?"

"I want to hold her hand again. Listen to her heart beat." Grant nodded. "You're right, of course. The old bitch will probably kill me."

"Is that why you left the notes?"

"Just a precaution, Lewis. Just figuring the odds. I like to be prepared."

Grant pulled a bag from the waterproof compartment and started walking up to the grass.

"Got a tent?" Lewis asked. "I can carry it."

"No tent. Got a light sleeping bag and a blue tarp. This little bag is the whole shebang. There's a whitefish in the boat. Caught it about an hour ago. Bring it up and I'll make us some dinner."

"Did you hear about Weegwasi? The old man just showed up again. After all that time and effort, he just shows up out of nowhere."

"I hadn't heard," Grant said.

"Yup. I drove out there a few weeks ago to check on him, and there he was, pretty as you please. Acted like nothing had ever happened. I asked him where he had been and he just shrugged his shoulders. I asked him about some *wiindigoog* chasing him and he says if a *wiindigoog* had chased him, it would have killed him and eaten him. So I just warned him about feeding wolves and left. Went home and wiped my white board clean. Does that beat everything or what?

"That beats everything, Lewis. How about boiled fish, potatoes and onions?"

"Sounds really good, but I don't want to leave you short of food."

"I can catch a nice trout tomorrow. It's three more days, I figure, to the grocery store at Ontonagon. I'll have to start carrying more food because I can't keep up this pace. I'll need a rest day now and then. My shoulders and arms are in open revolt."

"Are you really going to try to do the whole lake?"

"Lewis, I started this trip. That's all I can do. Nobody knows how anything will turn out."

"The mosquitos will eat you alive if the lake doesn't kill you first."

"Big hatch of dragonflies three days ago. Didn't you notice?"

"Sam, it's not the sort of thing I register."

"Well, look around you. Dragonflies will clean out the mosquitoes in a few days. They're pretty much gone already."

Radisson looked around, and suddenly he was aware of the big, helicopter-like bugs darting here and there.

"They may be the world's greatest predator," Sam said. "Every one of them has about 50,000 eyes. He sees everything in every direction. And he can instantly fly up, down, left, right or backward. He can hover, too. He'll eat absolutely anything he can find. In the water, he'll eat small fish."

"And right now they are eating all the mosquitoes?"

"Each one eats hundreds a day. Back in the dinosaur days, dragonflies were big as seagulls. There are fossils with two-foot wingspans."

"Imagine what the mosquitoes must have looked like."

"Imagine."

"Is there something I can do for you, Sam? Bring you something?"

"No, sir." Grant patted his waterproof bag. "I've got everything but hot and cold running water."

"Jackie is worried about you. What will I tell her?"

"That I am fine. And thank you very much, my dear, dear friends."

"I'll tell her that at least you're staying near shore."

"I have to. I'm an old man in a kayak. I get leg cramps. And I have to pee every two or three minutes."

Radisson scrounged wood and built a small fire. They sat on the bench of a picnic table in the gathering darkness, and ate a simple dinner. They talked and laughed together, and remembered many good times, back before Sam's memory went bad.

The wind fell away and the water in the harbor and the great lake laid down until it looked like black oil. Across it, the half-moon painted a white ribbon. In the extraordinary stillness of evening, they talked more softly until they stopped altogether.

"You better head home," Grant whispered. "You have a long way, and some of it is bad road."

"Yeah, I suppose. You okay? Lots of bears around here, coming down from the Porkies."

"I'm fine. Thanks."

Radisson bowed his head and said nothing for several minutes.

"It's been a hard year, Sam. For everybody. The pandemic and all. The isolation. A good many of us didn't make it through. Almost eight thousand of us in Wisconsin alone. That's like three World Trade Centers. But that may not be the worst part."

"I don't think it is."

"The strife. The anger. The division. I'll be honest with you, Sam. I'm disappointed in our politics."

"It's not a problem with the politics, Lewis. It's a problem with the species."

"You got that right. It's disappointing. The people weren't… well, we weren't what I had hoped."

"We're an unsuccessful genus, Lewis. A short-term evolutionary dead-end. There have been more than a dozen species of homo on this planet. Some were seven feet tall, stronger and had bigger brains. None of them lasted even a million years. We're the only ones left."

"Probably the bugs will finish us."

"More likely we will go extinct for the reason most species go extinct. Habitat destruction. Everything we do is unsustainable. When the oil is gone, the rare earth minerals, the water and soil, we'll leave without a trace."

"Probably."

"Or maybe Aayaash will burn us all out. Maybe we'll do it ourselves."

"And you'd be okay with that?"

"I have no say in it."

"You think you can fall in love again with this crazy, crazy world?" Radisson whispered.

"I'll start with this lake, the big shining lake of my people. We'll see."

"I'll come right out with it, Sam. You're past seventy and in poor health. I don't think you can survive this kayak trip. Even if you do okay for few weeks, when you get up there in Canada, in those northern waters, and you're fifty miles from the nearest house … I think something bad will happen. Or you'll just wear out."

Grant didn't say anything. He just smiled and nodded.

"I think this big shining lake will kill you, Sam."

"She might, Lewis. She's a hard woman." He looked out past the dock toward the beach and endless pool of dark water beyond. The swells still glided in, and the sound of them breaking against the rocky shore was all that wore on the stillness.

The waves had risen in the distant reaches of the lake, where the east wind was strong, and in their youth they had been tall and vigorous. Now even the mightiest fell over itself and slid away to nothing against the sand and small stones.

"It's a one-way trip," Grant said. "Wish it weren't, but it is."

"Don't do this, Sam."

"Look out there, Lewis. Listen to her. My God, she can be beautiful. So beautiful. And I want one more kiss."

EPILOGUE

JACOB AND JANICE sat together on the port-side gunnel, trying to counterbalance the north wind in the sail and the heel it created.

Janice had come to Red Cliff for the July holiday to visit her old co-workers, and to see if there was anything to be discovered about a relationship she had once had with a good-looking tribal policeman. It was a relationship aborted almost as soon as it had begun, his and her obligations pulling them in different directions.

When they stepped into the big Catalina, she smiled and her bright blue eyes sparkled. She called it a voyage of discovery. Jacob called it a test run. He was a careful man.

It was a warm morning with good wind, good enough to lift five tons of fiberglass and make it feel light as a butterfly with wings of silk. They had moved from the seat to the gunnel and leaned back against the railing.

Dewberry had the mainsheet pulled tight in a beam reach, and the starboard rail was nearly in the water.

"Where did you learn to sail?" she asked.

"Mr. Grant is teaching me. But we've been out enough times already that he trusts me with his boat. We've been going out pretty much every week since May. Even when it was cold."

"I'm surprised he's well enough to sail."

"He's fine. All the symptoms he had from the stroke are gone. He's working out. Building up his body. He's looking good, really. Nothing like when you saw him. He went to Illinois this week to meet his wife. Then he went kayaking."

"I didn't know he was married."

"She lives in Chicago. They don't see a lot of each other. They lost their only daughter. I guess she was shot in Milwaukee when she was a college student there."

"How terrible."

"I guess it kind of ruined things between them."

"What do you two talk about when you sail together?"

"You'd laugh."

"No. What? I want to know."

"He tells me a lot of old Ojibwe stories—the legends, you know. The same ones I learned as a child, but different because he tells them in a way that's more adult. It's kind of fun, actually. The stories aren't just entertainment for kids. They are a thousand years old and they carry down the wisdom of the Ojibwe people. We didn't have writing, so we recorded things in stories."

She laughed. "He's teaching you to be a witch doctor."

"He's okay. Not like a lot of people think. He tells me various roots and stuff that make medicines. But he explains how and why they work. He's scientific about it, not creepy."

She put her arm through his. "Does he have a love potion?" She giggled.

"I'll ask. He tells me so much stuff, I don't know how I'll remember it. A lot of it I record on my phone and then later I make notes. He tells me not to worry, that when the time comes, I'll remember what I need to."

"You don't believe those stories are true, do you, that Sky Woman fell through a hole in the sky or that Wenebojo talked to the geese?"

Jacob laughed. "Mr. Grant says only a white person would ask such a question. You have history books and newspapers and juries. You think truth is one little thing that can be wrung out of a pile of evidence. But truth is not a little thing. It is bigger than the whole pile. If you look too close you will never see it. What you need to know, he says, is that in these stories there is truth. You have to go find it."

They skimmed across the channel from Bayfield into the lee of Madeline Island. The sails relaxed and the boat flattened. The two young people moved back to the seats, and Janice bent at the waist to look down the open companionway into the cabin below. "We're spending the night on this thing?"

"Yes, ma'am. Unless we don't."

She laughed. "That's so like you. You always give a girl a way out. Is there room for both of us?" Her look was inquiring and slightly naughty.

"Mr. Grant used to live on this boat. It's 30 feet. Quite roomy, actually. You'll see. It has a nice galley. We'll cook dinner. I brought whitefish from the commercial fisherman in Cornucopia."

"I have a bikini on under my tank and shorts. Dare I, at any point, show it off?"

"Is this a test of willpower? Be careful. I might fail."

She laughed and Jacob suddenly pulled off his T-shirt and lay back in the sun, his bronze chest smooth and hard.

"Oh my," she said.

He looked at her naked arms and silky skin, her bright smile that seemed to be molded into her face, and those wonderful blue eyes. "Now I remember why I filmed you the first time I saw you."

"I think it was so cool you drove all the way to Eau Claire for my graduation," she said. "It was such a surprise when I saw you there. I thought you had forgotten all about me."

"I think about you all the time. I wanted to be there on a day I knew you would always remember. That way you'd remember me, too."

"That's very romantic. I'm sorry we didn't have any time. I was leaving on a last family vacation right after the ceremony. My job started the next Monday."

"It was perfect. I just wanted to say hello."

"And see if I had a boyfriend, maybe? See if I'd been lying to you? Jacob Dewberry, you are a careful man."

"It was nice to meet your parents. Nice people."

"Yes, they are. They were impressed by you."

They sailed around the Madeline Island breakwater and into the bay at La Pointe. They tied up at the restaurant there for a late breakfast. The wind was good all day, so they sailed on to Stockton Island, arriving at Presque Isle Bay in the late afternoon. It was a wild island in the government preserve, and home to the highest concentration of black bears in America. The only development was a ranger station, a dock, a tent camping area, and miles of trails. The dock was full of holiday powerboaters, so Jacob and Janice dropped anchor in the bay and took Grant's little tow-behind skiff to shore.

They walked across the spit to the beautiful, curving beach at Julian Bay, then stripped to their swimsuits and swam out over the wreck of the *Noquebay*. The old timber schooner had caught fire and run ashore there in 1905, before the rising lake level buried her in three fathoms of crystal-clear water.

They lay on the beach, and Jacob told her about Weegwasi and the plane crash. She gushed with questions.

"How did Sam Grant know the old man was alive?"

"I don't know. Intuition, I guess."

"How did he find him in that hole?"

"I don't know."

"How did he know the grandson was the *wiindigoog?* I thought the blood was from someone unrelated."

"He had studied the family pictures on the piano. He could see that that the grandson looked a lot like his mother, but not at all like his father, who would have been Weegwasi's son. That's not unusual on the reservation."

"Who was the Russian in the plane? Was it that Dubcek guy?"

"No, his accountant. I guess he was flying in every quarter to audit books. That's what he had in the briefcase."

"Accounting stuff?"

"Dubcek couldn't do anything in U.S. cash. He had a deal going with this Douglass Kincaid, who owned a big house on the lake. Dubcek put all the revenues from his rackets into Kincaid's fake pharmaceutical company in exchange for stock. It wasn't really a fake company, but it was just a half-dozen researchers working on something, not the big deal the papers thought it was. Several times a year Kincaid sent a lot of money to Russia to buy supplies and equipment that weren't real. Sometimes he'd buy stock back from the Russian company in U.S. currency. It was just a big money-laundering scheme."

Jacob smiled. "The accountant met Kincaid every three months in his big lake house and they'd go over the books together. That big briefcase spelled out everything."

"Have they caught Dubcek?"

"Nope. I don't think he would ever come to America. He stays in Canada when he's inspecting his North American businesses."

"How about Kincaid?"

"He was staying on some Caribbean Island. He took off when the FBI closed in, so he's on the run. They'll catch him."

"I'm proud of you," Janice said. "Sam Grant, too. That's really something."

The sun settled onto the big hills to the west, and the two sunbathers gathered their things and hurried back.

"Oh gosh, I haven't been to a campfire program since I was a little girl," Janice said. She danced ahead of Dewberry on the trail back, stopping occasionally to take his hand and pull him forward. "Let's go. It's almost dark."

Someone had built a big fire in the naturalist circle near the water on Anderson Point, just down the hill from the ranger station. There were a few rows of wooden benches around the fire and a handful of campers already waiting. Janice and Jacob snuggled onto an empty bench and turned their faces to the warm glow.

"Sam Grant and I were on this island in late May," Dewberry whispered. "Except we tied up at Quarry Bay. We walked the trail to Trout Point and camped there for the night."

"Oh, my goodness. He MUST be getting into shape."

"Yeah. It's about eight miles each way, with backpacks. He struggled to keep up with me, but he did. He wanted to go because he said he wanted to tell me some special stories. He said he had figured out what Sky Woman knew. She's part of an Ojibwe legend about the beginning of earth and the Ojibwe people."

"I've heard all about that. So… what did she know?"

"Jack squat."

"What?"

"That's what he said. He said his father, Standing Bear, gave him the answer. Sky Woman knew jack squat.

"You mean she knew nothing?"

"He said she didn't know how the world would turn out. Nobody does. He said she left her children here just hoping for the best."

"Uh-huh."

"He said that when you buy a house, it can burn down."

"Sure."

"He said that when you begin a marriage, or a family, or a business or anything else, you can't know how it will end. And you can't control the end, no matter how hard you try. He said the whole world was made by people who had no idea what they were doing. It was made without a plan or a purpose. He said we're all on a big round rock hurtling through space at 67,000 miles an hour, and nobody is driving.

"But he said that was fine, because the plan would fall apart anyway. He said that's the physics of the world. Plans fall apart. He said it is called entropy. He said Sky Woman knew about that."

"I know about that. Entropy is the lack of predictability in a system. It's the law in science that says disorder and randomness increase over time and never decrease."

"He talked about all those big cathedrals in Europe. It took hundreds of years to build them. The guys who laid the foundation stones had no idea how they would turn out. It took a century to build Notre Dame."

"And it almost burned down," Janice added

"Exactly. The point is, they began it. People took a leap of faith and started something they could never see finished. That's what he wanted me to know. We begin things. That's what we do. Like Sky Woman, we begin the world, brand new, every day. And we leave it to our children. We hope for the best. We don't know how anything will turn out. We could burn it all down."

"That's pretty dark, Jacob Dewberry."

"That's what I told him. But he just laughed. For a long time. He finally said, 'No, Jacob. Don't you see? We get to begin things. It's our role. It's our purpose. I buy the house. I marry the woman. I have the child. Maybe it all turns out badly, but the beginning was beautiful. All I can do is the beginning. I can begin something new this very day. On the last week of my life, I can begin a love affair with a woman I knew many years ago. On his last day, Aayaash created a robin.'"

"Beginnings. That's what we do," Jacob summarized. It's all we do, but it's the best part. We get to do the best part.

"He said he finally figured out what faith is. It's not believing that everything will be great at the end. It's living so that you know you did everything you could, that you started good things in the time you had, to the best of your ability."

It was inky dark now, except for the light of the big fire. Around the shore, the nightly symphony began. The sound of the gentle waves rolling up the gravel beach and then rattling back. The chitchat of banjo frogs, and somewhere far off, a bullfrog. The night birds joined in. The heron and the thrush and the killdeer. And of course, an owl. The air buzzed with the electric snap of invisible insects and the whine of cicada looking for love.

Jacob smiled. "The cicada sound desperate," he whispered. "Time is short. They only have one day."

Janice took his hand in both of hers and squeezed it. She leaned against him, letting him feel the nearness of her breast. The fire crackled and launched sparks into the darkness.

The naturalist came crunching down from the cabin above. Only the sound of his boots came at first, and then he merged into the firelight, a round red face, smiling. "Well, it looks like everyone is here who is coming," he said. "Why don't we begin?"

Janice looked into Dewberry's soft brown eyes, lit by the fire. "Yes," she whispered. "Why don't we?"